Books by Gilbert B. Cross

A Hanging at Tyburn
Mystery at Loon Lake

Mystery
at
Loon Lake

Mystery
at
Loon Lake

GILBERT B. CROSS

ATHENEUM   1986   NEW YORK

Atheneum
Macmillan Publishing Company
866 Third Avenue, New York, NY 10022

Type set by Maryland Linotype, Baltimore, Maryland
Printed and bound by Fairfield Graphics, Fairfield, Pennsylvania
Designed by Marjorie Zaum

10 9 8 7 6 5 4 3 2 1

Library of Congress Cataloging in Publication Data

Cross, Gilbert B.
Mystery at Loon Lake.

SUMMARY: When three friends explore an old, man-made
tunnel in the cliff beyond the swamp, they disturb someone
who then attempts to murder them.
[1. Mystery and detective stories] I. Title.
PZ7.C88252My   1986   [Fic]   86-3310
ISBN 0-689-31303-9

For
Peggy, John, Robert
and
for Agnes P.

Contents

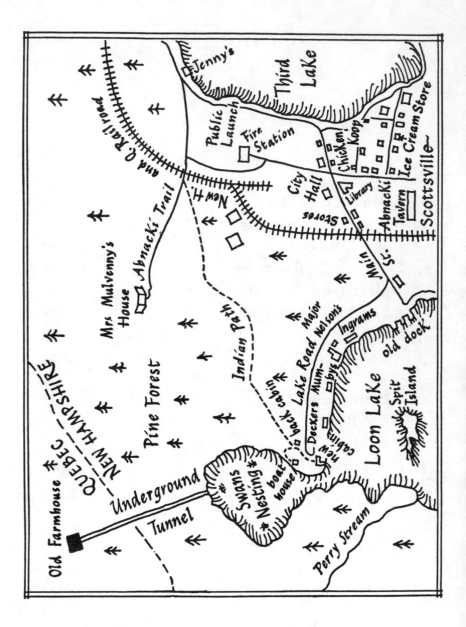

Mystery
at
Loon Lake

1

Bandit Spooks Us

Every summer as long as I can remember, the Glover family—that's us—stayed up at Loon Lake in northern New Hampshire. We were just this side of the Canada-United States border, surrounded by pine forests. It wasn't the place where you'd expect someone to try to kill you, that's for sure.

My mom wasn't with us this summer. She plays first violin in the New Hampshire Symphony, and I guess she's kind of famous. She's also pretty good when it comes to surprises too. Last fall, while touring Japan, she found a brother for me—a Vietnamese orphan called Nguyen (you don't pronounce the "g" in his name). We're both twelve; he's a month older, but I'm an inch taller.

Nguyen doesn't say much though his English is pretty good, and he speaks Japanese, French and Vietnamese. He's light years ahead of my natural brother, Rodney, who's as much of a pest as any seven-year-old can be. I just know I was never seven, and I know I didn't go around calling everything "sweet" or "gross."

I guess I'm rambling on, but when I get to telling what happened in the Swamp, things will get a lot simpler.

I was glad to have Nguyen around because Dad was forever writing books. When he lit up his pipe, you knew another book was on the way. On went the word processor and off went the rest of the world. The latest book was about some Roman emperor called Titus. He was emperor for only two years; then, he died of a fever. Boy!

Nguyen and I liked to swim in Loon Lake before breakfast. When the schoolbell rang, that was Dad's signal for breakfast. When he got writing, he sometimes forgot to ring the bell, and once he forgot to make breakfast, lunch, and dinner.

Nguyen dived down just as the bell rang. I waited for him to come up. He could stay down for almost two minutes. When he popped up, he had a rock in his hand. "Find a rock," he said, showing it to me.

I looked it over as we made our way up the short path to the cabin. Nguyen looked dry already. "Ugly cuss, isn't it," I said. "Some kid tried to carve a face on it."

"He need practice," said Nguyen, grinning and wiping it dry with his towel.

We crossed the redwood deck and went in through the kitchen door. This was the main cottage where Dad and Rodney stayed. Nguyen and I were in the back cabin so we wouldn't disturb Dad's writing. The back cabin was a quarter of a mile up the hill and had been my grandfather's cottage.

Nguyen used his rock to prop up one end of a shelf of books. There were books everywhere, some still uncrated.

Dad had made biscuits. They were a bit burned, and the scrambled eggs stuck to the pan, but no one said much about that. One day he'd made French toast without using any eggs.

Dad left us to it. Already, clutching a cup of coffee, he was gazing at the words on the screen. He always dressed the same way when he was writing. Suede shoes, old jeans, and a gray or wine-colored sweat shirt with a hood.

Outside, there was a hoot from the van that takes Rodney to his day camp. Dad couldn't look after him and write; you can't write a book and be popping up every minute to see if Rodney was drowning or wandering in the poison ivy.

Rodney rushed off carrying his old fishing pole and swim trunks. He stuck out his tongue at me as he left. I ignored him.

When Nguyen and I had finished eating, I told Dad we were going swimming. He grunted, staring intently at the screen of his word processor.

"Rodney fell into the poison ivy, Dad," I added "and there's a shark in the lake."

He grunted again. I looked at Nguyen and shrugged, but just as we were leaving Dad said, "Look out for bloodthirsty Indians, too, while you're out there."

That's Dad's sense of humor for you.

It was a pretty steep climb up to the back cottage. It was on one of the trails the Abnacki Indians had used ages ago, and some years before it had had the best view of Loon Lake in the county. It was on a sort of promontory that divided the lake from what we called the Swamp. There were steep trails down to both. The Swamp wasn't really a swamp. It was a very shallow area at the north end of Loon Lake, covered with small islands of sand, reeds and tall grass. Narrow channels crisscrossed it, but they were seldom more than two feet deep. There was a winding passage from the back cabin down to the Swamp. It hugged the side of a cliff, then flattened out to a narrow beach and the old boathouse.

The back cabin was pretty big considering; there was a rear room with two beds in it, a bathroom and a big kitchen and dining area. The front room had a large picture window. A redwood deck ran along the south side and half the length of the west wall to the side door.

Years ago, when the area had been cleared, someone planted fruit trees, and you could still get apples and pears if Rodney didn't eat them first.

Another thing; I hate to admit this, but it could get kind of scary up there. Things *moved* in the night. You know what I mean? You're lying there on your bed trying to sleep, and things move around. I'm talking about rustling in the undergrowth or sudden movements you sense if you suddenly look out of a window. Of course there's no way to tell anyone about it because they would just pooh-pooh the idea. Dad would have made some joke about the ghosts of the Abnaki Indians, and Rodney, well you can just guess. He was with Dad, secure behind deadbolt locks and an alarm system in the main cottage.

"Get suit?" asked Nguyen.

"Sure," I said, rummaging in my dresser until I found a pair that fitted. Dad never thought about things like clothes. When Mom got back she'd march us all down to Dever's store, Dad and all, and buy everything we needed.

I threw my trunks onto the patchwork quilt on my bed and opened the bathroom door to get a towel. As I did so there was a sudden movement. A towel with a blue border tore through the gap, just above the floor, banged into my legs, fell back, then began rolling over the carpet. Nguyen let out a shout and jumped onto the sofa. The towel stopped, turned round, then moved off

7

in another direction. Next it slammed up against the wall, grunted, and rolled over, sprouting four black and grey legs.

"Bandit!" I shouted. "It's Bandit!"

"Bandit?" said Nguyen. "Oh boy, he sure scare me."

"And me," I said, to make him feel better.

The towel got tangled around the leg of the sofa and out of one end scurried a thoroughly frightened wild raccoon. He shot across the floor and bumped up against the screen door with a thud.

"Let him out," I said, "but be careful."

Nguyen edged to one side, stepped down off the sofa and picked up the broom. Bandit seemed dazed; his chest heaved up and down.

"Careful now," I warned Nguyen; "he's only winded." I didn't want an angry Bandit taking a lump out of either of us.

Nguyen pushed on the screen door with the broom. Bandit looked up at the broom handle, then Nguyen.

"Scat," I shouted. "Get lost, Bandit."

The door was open about six inches, and when Bandit felt the outside air on his fur he turned around and was gone. The door slammed behind him.

I stared at my brother. "Phew! That was something else." Outside the only sound was the crickets and grasshoppers. Bandit had scuttled off home. A bee suddenly blundered into the screen and let out a loud buzz. Both of us jumped. Nguyen let out his breath in a long, slow whistle. "Well it no ghost, only a raccoon."

Bandit was a real pesky animal. From the tip of his inquisitive nose to the end of his bushy ringed tail, Bandit was one mean raccoon. For one thing, he had no sense of gratitude. Last year, I had found him with his head stuck in a beer can. He'd been sticking his nose in where it wasn't wanted and pushed too hard. I tried to grab him, but he scratched me on the arm. Then I tried to catch him in a cardboard box, but he ripped it up with his claws before I could get him in it. Then I finally lost my temper, got my baseball bat and whacked the can with it. Bandit's "helmet" crunched up and off; he let out a loud squeal and rushed between my legs into the pines.

Dad wasn't happy with what we'd done. We were told to steer clear of raccoons. "They look cute," he said, "but they've got teeth like razors and claws to match. And there's always the chance of rabies." (Dad has a thing about rabies.) "And besides Major Nelson won't like it."

Major Nelson was a retired Marine who had a cottage three doors from ours. He hated raccoons and was always trying to run them off. Unfortunately Bandit now hung around our back cabin all the time, hoping for a handout.

"You save someone's life, you responsible for him,"

said Nguyen when I had introduced him to Bandit. "Chinese proverb."

That was enough excitement for one day. We spent the rest of it swimming. But I guess by then I was thoroughly spooked. Several times when I looked toward the shore, I thought I saw bright flashes as if someone was watching us through binoculars. I mean, it didn't happen all the time so it couldn't have been a broken bottle or anything like that. But it was crazy, why should anyone be watching us? It didn't make any sense.

2

Someone Is Watching

That night Dad seemed to be in a good mood; he'd finished an important chapter in his book. He had decided Titus's brother had poisoned him so he could be emperor. So that night we had a fire outside the cabin and roasted marshmallows. And he told one of his ghost stories. We sat there, our sticks in the fire and flavored marshmallows turning to sweet hot goo.

"This happened just a few miles away." began Dad. "about five years ago. I remembered it well. My sister Gertrude lived just over the border in Quebec, a small town by the name of Bellefeville. Well, this one day, she came to see us. We only had the back cabin then."

He paused and twirled his stick. The marshmallow

sagged in the middle, and he drew the stick towards him and popped the creamy stuff into his mouth.

"Boy, that's good," he said, wiping his hand on the grass.

"Well, your Aunt Gertrude stayed with us a couple of nights, then started back home. She stopped in Chartierville to visit with a friend and stayed late gossiping. When she realized the time, she got to her car and left in a big hurry. Right away she sees this car behind her, headlights blazing. By now, it was almost midnight, and she was frightened because that's a very isolated stretch of road."

Dad stopped. Rodney's marshmallows had caught fire. The flames reflected in his glasses.

When Rodney was settled and a new marshmallow speared, Dad began again.

"So Gertrude blowtorches the pedal to the metal" (that's Dad's idea of the way kids talk today), "and starts running the lights of all the little towns on the way.."

He slapped at the side of his face as if a mosquito had landed there. All of us kids jumped, even though it was a favorite trick of his.

"No one was so glad to see her home as Gertrude was. She zoomed into her driveway and roared right into the garage, keeping her hand on the horn. Your Uncle Jules came running to see what was going on."

He looked at Nguyen, who giggled like a nerd.

"The other car," continued Dad, "slowly pulled right in the driveway. The driver got out.

" 'What's the racket all about?' shouted Jules. 'The whole neighborhood's awake.'

" 'This man followed me,' said Gertrude, almost in tears. 'He followed me twenty miles.'

"The stranger took off his hat. " 'It's true.' he said. 'I did follow, but there's a reason. I was just getting out of work when I heard a man had been seen around the parking lot who resembled the maniac who escaped from the mental asylum.'

'You mean the man with the hook.'

"Right. He has a metal hook instead of a right hand. I turned on my headlights and I thought I saw a man's head bob down in your back seat.' "

Somewhere in the pines, I heard an owl hoot mournfully. The Abnaki Indians believed that meant someone would die soon. Rodney's marshmallow had fallen into the fire, but we ignored it.

" 'There's only one way to find out,' said Jules; 'we must take a look.'

"Gertrude began protesting, but the two men went to the rear of the car and there . . .

"What?" squeaked Rodney, "what?"

"There, hanging from the back door handle, dripping with blood, was a large metal hook."

There was a long silence. Then Dad laughed and slapped at another mosquito. "Sleep well, boys."

When we got back to the back cabin, Nguyen and I jammed a chair against the main door and wedged the kitchen door with a stick. I knew Rodney would be happy sleeping in the main cabin with Dad, while we were stuck back in the woods.

Jamming the doors made me feel a bit better, but I sure couldn't sleep. All the night sounds that you don't normally hear because they're always there came in loud and clear. Crickets chirped, and bullfrogs croaked in the Swamp. Even the electric clock hummed loudly enough to be heard.

"Nguyen, you asleep?"

There was no answer.

I lay there thinking it was a pity we couldn't close our ears the way we could our eyes. Then there was a new sound. At first it was very faint and distant—the throb of a small trolling motor—the kind used for bass fishing.

The wind, or whatever, must have been just right; I followed the engine's progress across the lake. It seemed to be getting closer. That could mean only one thing; the boat was going to leave the lake and enter the narrow channel leading into the Swamp.

"Nguyen," I said, "wake up."

Nothing happened so I got out of bed and reached over and shook him. "Wake up."

He rolled to the far side of the bed, and I had to

14

reach across and shake him. This time it worked. Mumbling something in Vietnamese, he sat up.

"Get up," I said; "there's a boat going into the Swamp."

I don't know why I was so concerned about it. Was I afraid the crew would get into trouble? No one takes a boat in there usually because the long grass and weeds can foul an engine. But there wasn't any real danger; the water seldom got more than a few feet deep. Still I was wide awake, and now I'd wakened Nguyen. I couldn't just tell him to forget it. Besides I was curious. Who would take a boat into the Swamp at midnight?

For a while I couldn't find both sneakers. When I did, one looked as if a certain raccoon had chewed on it. Again I resolved to search for Bandit's secret entrance; I didn't want him chewing my toes one night. Nguyen had his flashlight. He tried it; the batteries were OK.

The path down to the Swamp is pretty rough. Dad didn't like us using it in the daytime, let alone at night, but when there's a moon shining, it's safe enough.

The back cabin is on a cleared lot with the fruit trees around it. The path goes down steeply for fifty yards then turns and hugs the side of the cliff. It's narrow, so we had to go single file. Above, the cliff face rose almost vertically into the air.

At the foot of the cliff was a pine thicket that went almost to the water's edge. Small animals scurried around us, disturbed by our unexpected presence. The bullfrogs were alternately silent and deafening. There was that damp earthly smell you get at night, like someone burning leaves. It was much darker among the pine trees, but I knew the way. When the ground became springy underfoot, we were almost at the boathouse. The water looked black and cold, but it was about ten degrees warmer than Loon Lake. Water was oozing out of the ground into our footsteps as we approached the boathouse. Once there was a slight splash, and I caught sight of a small head above water and a zigzagging tail behind.

"Water snake," I muttered to Nguyen.

The boat's engine was muffled by the islands. I listened carefully, but couldn't get any idea of the direction. When we'd been above the Swamp, the sound was clear enough. Now, on the same level, sounds didn't travel so far.

"We get out the boat?" asked Nguyen.

The canoe was a real Indian canoe purchased by Dad from an old Pennacook Indian.

"Sure," I replied. "Maybe we can find them."

The boathouse had lost its doors five winters ago; they'd been torn off and thrown thirty feet during a gale. When Dad heard this, he sighed and said, "Well, that's that." He used the timber from them to plug the gaps in the walls.

Beside the canoe, there wasn't anything much of value in the boathouse. It was full of old junk that had been piled in the corners and on hanging shelves Dad put up the time he thought he'd write a book about John Paul Jones. There were paint pots with dried up cakes of paint, some ratty old ropes, a broken oar or two and several green trash bags where Dad put the manuscripts of books after they were finally published. He couldn't bear to burn them. His old bicycle hung from a hook on the wall, and there were two empty violin cases stuck back in the far corner. It was an awful mess, and Dad was forever saying it had to be cleaned up. Then he'd get the idea for a book and forget everything else.

There was a set of rollers in the middle of the floor. All you had to do was get the canoe on them and push. In theory any boat would slide easily into the water. Years ago the rollers had rusted and started sticking; now it was a bit of a struggle to drag the boat into the water.

In the Swamp you're never more than a few feet from a small sandbar or island. Tall grass grows everywhere and around the edges of the little islands grow enormous reeds. The water channels between the islands are usually very narrow. Really, it's like a maze, and we didn't have any way of knowing where the boat was.

Finally we stopped paddling and sat there. I was shivering and wishing I'd brought a heavy jacket, when Nguyen tensed and whispered, "Over there."

"I can't hear anything."

"Small motor, heading to the left."

You don't argue with someone like Nguyen; his ears are like a bat's. I dipped my paddle overboard being careful not to make any more noise than necessary.

Pretty soon I heard the sound of the trolling motor. It grew louder, then began to fade as it drew away from us.

Every time we slid between the giant bullrushes, they made a crackling sound that must have been audible miles away. I whispered to Nguyen. "They can hear us for sure."

"Think not," he whispered, pausing. "Engine shuts out other noises. We safe if not seen."

If you can have a game of hide and go seek with only one side playing, that's what we had. We would shoot out from behind the reeds, see nothing, and slide deep into another bunch of them. Then we stared out at the expanse of dark water ahead of us hoping to catch a glimpse of the boat.

We'd been out over an hour before we got lucky. Coming out from behind one island, we heard the sound of the engine and saw the stern of a boat vanishing into a forest of reeds. Three men were visible, but only for an instant.

If we hadn't seen them, we'd never have found the channel. It twisted and turned, and there were times when we couldn't see more than a few feet at a time. Fortunately it was night, so the mosquitoes weren't out in force. At dusk they would have eaten us alive.

We eased our way through the reeds. I was in the bow. Every so often a black, wet reed would slap me in the face and shower me with water.

"Can't hear boat any more," said Nguyen, behind me. "Maybe we lost them."

I didn't think so. For one thing, the Swamp narrowed at the northern tip. Ahead was the land, rising a hundred feet above us, and pine forests stretching for miles.

"Keep heading north," I whispered. "They've got to be going in that direction."

Nguyen grunted. I heard his paddle slice the water. Just ahead of me, a water rat swam across from one island to another leaving a tiny wake behind him.

Then, suddenly, the reeds parted and ahead of us was the edge of the Swamp, the cliff rising almost vertically. A mass of ferns grew at the water's edge.

"Nothing," I said in disgust. "We've lost them."

"We turn?" asked Nguyen.

I grunted. There was enough space to turn the canoe. I began paddling, and the boat turned slowly until the stern was brushing the ferns at the water's edge.

"Stop," said Nguyen. "There's a beer bottle here."

"So what?" I said over my shoulder.

"How come this bottle here?"

That was a good question. It wasn't likely to have come from anywhere except the boat we'd been following. You don't picnic on the side of a cliff.

The canoe slid backwards. I twisted and watched as he tried to knock it towards us. Instead the bottle floated away towards the cliff face and vanished into a huge patch of ferns.

"Come on," I said; "we've lost them, and we're wasting time."

Nguyen poked at the ferns once more. His oar disappeared out of sight.

"There's a big hole here, Jeff," he called out.

With that I back-paddled with Nguyen's help until we were facing the hole. The boat slid forward parting the undergrowth like a giant green curtain; the ferns brushed over me as I passed through. I felt the cold air and the smell of stagnant water as we entered a cavern whose size I had no way of guessing because the moonlight could not penetrate the ferns. One thing was certain, once beyond the entrance, the cavern widened considerably, and the roof was much higher. It was scary all right; it was exciting too.

Nguyen's flashlight snapped on. As our eyes adjusted, we could see solid rock walls on each side.

"Shine it up," I said, "and turn in your seat."

The beam traced its way up the sides to the roof above. My words bounced back from the walls and echoed in the enclosed space.

"It's a cave," said Nguyen. "They went into this cave."

"It's no cave," I said. "Look you can see drill marks on the wall. And look how regular it is."

It was a semi-circular tunnel rising twelve feet above the water. The echoes of the trolling motor receded into the distance. Nguyen's flashlight probed the darkness up ahead.

There was no sign of recent digging as far as I could tell. I saw no tools anywhere and no piles of rock to suggest anyone was still working down there.

Then I heard Nguyen chuckle. "Found bottle," he said leaning over the side of the canoe and fishing it out. "What's 'Guinness Stout' anyway?"

"Beats me," I said. "It looks like beer. Throw it back. If Dad sees that in the canoe he'll get the wrong idea."

Out it went.

"I'll paddle," I said, "you hold the light."

We moved slowly into the black depths ahead. The flashlight revealed nothing.

"I think I . . ." began Nguyen, but then the light fell from his hand into the canoe, and I was thrown forward on top of him.

"Gate there," said Nguyen, as we sorted ourselves out. "Blocks tunnel."

"Well that's that," I said, examining it with the flashlight. "It's solid iron bars, and the hinges are stuck into the rock." I pushed on it, but it wouldn't budge an inch. "No getting past that," I added, keeping the sense of relief out of my voice. I really didn't want to go any further. The smell reminded me of the day our sewers backed up.

We paddled out of there much faster than we paddled in. Nguyen had a sixth sense when it came to traveling by boat. He found the boathouse when I couldn't even tell what direction we were traveling.

As we were putting the canoe away, I dropped the flashlight. It needed a good sharp bang to get the light on again. Then I saw something that really shook me.

"Look at this," I said, pointing to a patch of mud.

Nguyen stooped.

"See here. There's the impression of one of our sneakers, and on top of it—"

"A man's shoe," said Nguyen. "Someone spy on us, maybe?"

"You better believe it," I said straightening up. "You better believe it."

3

Jenny Weber

The next morning, Dad forgot to make breakfast, and when Nguyen and I got to the main cabin, he was already at work; paper was unwinding from the printer, and he was sitting fascinated by it all. Rodney had left for camp.

"You guys will have to muddle through," he said. "I'm busy with the eruption of Mount Vesuvius."

"You mean Mount Vesuvius blew up while this guy Titus was emperor?" I asked, while fishing out a box of Rodney's favorite breakfast cereal, Boo-Berries.

"With one almighty bang," said Dad, almost rubbing his hands with glee. "Thousands covered with volcanic ash, cities wonderfully preserved."

I'll say this for Titus; life was never dull when he was around.

"We swim?" asked Nguyen, pouring himself a glass of chocolate milk.

"Later," I whispered. "I want to go to Scottsville. Maybe the library has something about the tunnel we were in. It must have caused a stir."

Nguyen nodded. He was always willing to fit in with my plans. I was curious. I mean why would anyone build a tunnel in the middle of nowhere? It didn't make sense.

We got out our bikes—mine was a ten speed—Nguyen had a dirt bike and zoomed along Lake Road. As we passed Major Nelson's cottage, I saw him loading brush onto a trailer. He glared at us because he figured we were feeding Bandit.

Where Main Street joins Lake Road you get the best view for miles. Directly opposite is Spit Island and the old Dr. Shatney mansion. Up to the north was the narrow neck of Loon Lake leading to the Swamp. Above on the east side was the back cabin, invisible because the white pines shielded it from view.

To the south was the canal that linked Loon Lake to the string of lakes and canals that went down to the Connecticut River and the Atlantic.

"Look, look," Nguyen said pointing and skidding to a stop as a flock of huge white swans began landing in the lake. Not one had a wingspan less than five feet.

"We better not feed them," said Nguyen. "Major Nelson get pretty mad."

"I know it," I replied, "besides they probably carry rabies."

Scottsville isn't much—two main streets, a dozen stores, a drugstore and a large house that served as a library. The streets crossed near the "City Hall," where the sheriff's post was located. Since there wasn't any crime, Deputy McGlynn had an easy time of it. That was probably why he weighed three hundred pounds. You could see him any day sitting at the Texaco station in a chair complaining to Mr. Johnson about the summer people. His son had a cabin on Lake Road.

Nguyen and I parked our bikes against the maple tree outside the library on Main and went in.

We didn't go there often. For one thing the librarian, Miss Boswell, was pretty ferocious. Nguyen was scared of her and called her "dragon lady," which I thought was pretty good.

As usual she was sitting at the return desk wearing a suit covered by a brown smock with the motto "Reading is Good for You." Her reading glasses were suspended by a silver chain around her neck. Behind her was one of those stained glass windows. Not the religious kind with the Crucifixion or Jonah and the Whale, but all sorts of colors. Her hair was green with a red topping. It looked like a colored beehive.

"Good morning, boys," she said, her jaw tightening at the sight of us. "Please make sure your hands are clean before you touch the books."

We nodded and went into the main room. All the walls were covered by shelves except at the far end where there was a dusty moose's head.

She followed us in, of course.

"We want a book on the history of Loon Lake, please," I said.

Miss Boswell wasn't really listening. She had her eye on Nguyen who was looking at a *National Geographic*. The last time we were in, he had absent-mindedly swatted a fly with a copy. It was after that he'd come up with the name "Dragon Lady".

"History," I prompted her. "Of Loon Lake."

"Card catalog, Jeffrey. New Hampshire, history of, Scott County."

The 'N' file was missing. Looking back into the main room, I saw a girl sitting in the corner working carefully through the cards. She was taking notes with one of those giant ball-point pens with lots of colors.

I went over to her. She was about my age and had on shorts and a T shirt. The front of her shirt had a picture of Frankenstein's monster's head with two wires coming out of it. There was the usual scar and a bolt in the neck.

"Are you going to be long with that card file," I asked. "I just want to look up a book."

She just ignored me and kept on making a list of books.

"I won't be a minute," I continued. "Probably half a minute."

She looked up. "You're not from round here."

"No. We've got a cabin on the lake."

"Thought so." She flipped to the next card.

"Well?"

"Well what?"

"Can I use the file drawer?"

"What do you want to look up?"

Now that's just like a girl. Always sticking their noses in where they're not wanted.

"None of your business," I said.

"OK." She went back to her list.

This was embarrassing. I mean you can't just deck someone over a library book. And if I started a fight in the library, Miss Boswell would call the cops for sure. They would call dad.

"All right, I'll tell you."

She looked up and smiled. Just as I expected, she had braces.

"What's your name?"

"Jeff Glover. That's my brother, Nguyen."

She looked at him. "You've got two fathers?"

"My adopted brother. He's Vietnamese. Can I look for this book?"

"Tell me first."

"There's a tunnel underground in the Swamp. I wanted to find out who built it."

"There's no tunnel in the Swamp, you dope."

"Is so!"

"OK, OK, keep your fur on." She pushed the file drawer in my direction. "Be my guest."

I peeked in fast before she changed her mind. She was looking over my shoulder. Nosy.

"My name's Jenny Weber," she said. "I spend a lot of my time here because I'm going to be a brain surgeon, and they're the smartest people in the world."

I ignored her. There was one book listed—*Loon Lake Madness* by Elsie Mulvenny. Written across it was "Missing 5/Dec/81."

"Someone ripped it off," Jenny said. "Tough."

Nguyen and I left and sat outside on the bench under the big maple tree. Before Miss Boswell's time, according to Dad, people used to sit outside the library and read books. Now they had to be checked out first.

"Well look at you two," said Jenny Weber, coming out of the library with two thick books under her arm. "Cheerful, aren't we?" She placed her books on the library steps and sat down next to them. "You're not too smart—even for a boy."

"I'm as smart as you are," I snapped. "My IQ's one hundred twenty."

"If it was ninety, you'd know what to do." She stood

up, slapped the dust off the rear of her shorts, and said, "Come on!"

I was going to argue; I mean why should we be taking orders from some girl we didn't even know? But in the end we just tagged along. Jeez!

Pushing our bikes, we followed her for two blocks down Big Beaver before turning into a side street. Halfway along, Jenny opened a screen door into a small hardware store. On the far side was a counter, and above it, suspended from two chains, was a sign saying "38 Flavors of Ice Cream." We crossed the room; behind us the screen door crashed shut.

There were potted plants everywhere and ferns in baskets hanging from above. Jenny chose a little table with iron legs and a thick red table-cloth and picked up the menu.

"I like the Hot Fudge Fanatic, with the fudge on the side. You get more that way." She tossed her head, the blond ponytail shook. "We get two spoons, but I pour."

We ordered one Hot Fudge Fanatic and a Tin Roof. Since I don't like peanuts, she arranged to share that with Nguyen.

"I didn't even know this place was here," I said.

"'Course not. Summer people never know anything."

A bell rang.

"They're ready," said Jenny. "Go get them."

29

The ice creams cost three sixty. Nguyen had a dollar seventy-five; I found the rest—just. Jenny didn't have any money!

"You look, but you don't see," she said, carefully pouring fudge over the mountain of vanilla on her side.

"I don't . . ."

"Don't you know anyone called Mulvenny, dope?"

Lightening struck. "You mean—our Mrs. Mulvenny?"

"Who else? How many people do you know called Mulvenny? Bet you two bucks she's Elsie." She wiped ice cream from her mouth with a paper napkin.

"I don't have two more bucks," I answered. "Anyway we can't go up to the big house and ask for a book."

"Why not? I would."

"Wait a minute." I felt a bit dumb. "I mean. Well, what about—you know—the stories? Isn't she supposed to be a bit weird?"

"You mean all that stuff about her being a witch?" Jenny laughed. "All great people were considered crazy. Just because her husband drowned himself in the Swamp doesn't mean *she's* crazy, does it?"

"No," I admitted. "I've never met her."

"Neither have I, but now's the time. Anyway, as a scientist I don't believe in witches. So there."

I was no scientist, but no girl was going to show me up. "Let's go," I said.

4

Bickerstaffe, The Butler

Jenny didn't own a bike so we had to ride double on mine; it wasn't that bad. Naturally I did all the work pedaling while she sat on the saddle telling me about Mrs. Mulvenny.

"She's owned land around here for as long as my dad can remember, and he was born here."

"What's she look like?" I asked over my shoulder, puffing as we climbed Wild Rose Lane.

"Never seen her; no one has. She stays inside her house and never comes out. She's got a butler, though."

"A butler!"

"Right. A real English butler with a black suit and a derby hat."

We walked up Abnacki Trail, a long, narrow, un-
paved road that led to Mrs. Mulvenny's house.

"What does your mom do?" Jenny asked.

"She's the first violinist in the New Hampshire
Symphony."

"Wow!"

I pushed the bike; Jenny was thinking.

"What about your dad?"

"Teaches history. At the university."

"That's pretty impressive. 'Course it's not like playing in a symphony orchestra."

I stopped pushing for a moment. That hadn't oc-
curred to me.

Jenny had got a few steps ahead of me so I had to
catch up with her. "What do your parents do?"

"Dad's with U.S. Customs; he and Ma also run a
guest house near Third Lake. It helps pay the bills."

We left our bikes leaning against one of the gate-
posts," a big brick thing. The black iron gates were
locked, but there was enough space between the bars
for us to squeeze through.

It sure was a strange house, like that place in *Psycho
III*, which was just about the scariest movie I ever saw.
For one thing, it was all brick so it must have cost the
earth. The basic shape seemed to be a letter "V" and
where the two wings met in the middle there was a three
story tower. At both ends were tall chimneys, and along

part of the front was a widow's walk. That was real weird because you probably couldn't even see Loon Lake from it. You sure couldn't see the ocean.

Alongside the drive was a flagstone walk. The ground had come up like a volcano in parts and pushed the flags to one side. The lawn was overgrown, the hedges weren't trimmed, and lots of rose bushes had gone crazy, growing every which way. There had been flowerbeds on both sides of the walkway, but they were full of dead plants and cluttered with brown leaves.

"Nice place," commented Jenny.

The path stopped and we crossed the drive in front of the house. Sunk back in a deep entrance was the front door. It was dark because the light bulb over us was missing. There was one of those multicolored glass windows like the one in the library.

"No lights, shutters on the windows. This a pretty spooky place," said Nguyen.

Jenny wasn't quite so fast pooh-poohing this, but she did mutter something about the place needing a gardener and a coat of paint. Finally she said, "Find the bell and stop talking dumb."

We couldn't find any bell. That didn't faze Jenny. She took off one of her sneakers and banged on the door with it. The sound seemed to retreat into the depths of the house. Nguyen suddenly shivered. I felt him. Even

33

Jenny didn't look quite so sure of herself as she put her sneaker back on.

"It's just an old house," she muttered. "An old broken-down house."

I didn't hear a sound from inside the house, so when the door opened, I jumped. At least it didn't groan on its hinges.

The butler stood there exactly the way Jenny had described him, except he wasn't wearing his derby. He was no more than five feet tall and bald on top, but I'll bet he was the only man in Scottsville wearing a three piece suit with gray gloves. His eyes were too small, almost piggy; he was doing his best not to scowl too much. In fact his jaws were so prominent he seemed to have more of a muzzle than a face.

Jenny was taken aback by his sudden appearance. Above me I thought I heard a click.

"Madam's not at home," he said. His voice was high-pitched, which was sort of unexpected. You could sure hear the English accent.

"We'd like to speak to Mrs. Mulvenny, please," said Jenny not a bit scared.

"She don't see no visitors," he snapped, turning away and starting to close the door. "So hop it."

"Let them come up, Bickerstaffe," said a voice from above us.

"Very good, madam," said the butler suddenly sounding polite. There must have been a mike and a speaker in the wall above us. I heard the click when it went off. So did Bickerstaffe.

"Follow me, and keep yer thieving 'ands off of things," he said, leading the way down a long entrance hall. He seemed to glide across the floor; we almost had to run to keep up. When we came suddenly upon a wide oak staircase leading to the first floor, the butler went up without breaking his stride.

On the first landing was a long gallery with doors leading off it. Everything was paneled in dark wood, and everywhere there were boxes and boxes of stuff piled up against the walls. Each of them had a number on it. As far as I could see they all started with nineteen.

Bickerstaffe knocked on a set of large double doors. From within came a firm "Enter."

We all gaped as we entered the room. It was as big as Grand Central Station. Almost. Not so brightly lit, but I could see steps at the far end leading to a huge pipe organ.

Every inch of wall was covered with a painting of some sort. They'd all got kind of dark too, so the pictures all seemed to be sinking out of sight. They were mainly battle scences—horses charging, cannons going off, that kind of thing. There was lots of furniture, all of it covered by white painters' cloths, and along the walls were rows and rows of filing cabinets. Across the center of the room was a long wooden table piled up with cardboard boxes. Behind it sat Mrs. Mulvenny. She had hollowed out a space. Dotted around the table were various knick-knacks, such as a bust of Beethoven—the kind that glares at you.

"I'm Elsie Mulvenny," she said in a high, cracked voice. "I'm very busy, but you can stay for tea. I don't get too many visitors these days." She let out a few cackles. Sounding like an angry hen.

Then I realized she was sitting in a wheelchair. There was a humming noise as she drove down her side of the table. At the end she spoke into a microphone.

"Tea for four, Bickerstaffe, and no gingernut cookies."

"I hate gingernuts," she explained, driving along our side, but Bickerstaffe loves them. He calls them biscuits and buys them for himself."

Mrs. Mulvenny was dressed as if she expected to go West on a wagon train, except she didn't have a pioneer bonnet on.

"Pull that drape off," she told Nguyen. "There's a sofa under it . . ." She paused, then cackled, "I think."

There was. "Bingo," said Mrs. Mulvenny. "Not senile, yet. That sofa is a Queen Anne, but she won't mind." Then nothing happened for five minutes. We all stayed exactly where we were until Bickerstaffe carried in a little table with a teapot and cups. There were little cookies too!

"Eat up. You pour," she said to Jenny. "Tell me your names."

We told her. She looked closely at all of us, especially Nguyen. "You're a long way from home, boy," she said more to herself than us. "Vietnamese name, eh?" She was real old, at least sixty, with a face shrunk up like a dried apple, but her eyes twinkled. When she touched Nguyen's hand, he jumped back.

"Don't be afraid, boy. I went to Vietnam once. Beautiful place. Beautiful people. What do you know about income taxes?" she said, turning suddenly to me. "Eh?"

"Nothing much," I replied, panicking a bit.

"Pour more tea, Jenny." Then she muttered. "Typical. No one knows anything about taxes until they have to pay them. Well, what do you children want?" She munched on a cookie. "I'm very busy working on my 1939 tax return. I left out several deductions."

Mrs. Mulvenny pretty much filled my idea of a witch, but Jenny was amused by it all. She turned her face away to hide a smile. I kept thinking Mrs. Mulvenny would suddenly leap out of her wheelchair and pounce on me to see if I needed fattening up.

"It's about the Swamp," I said.

"Swamp. What Swamp?"

"The low-lying area to the north of Loon Lake," said Jenny, putting down her little china cup. I was scared stiff I'd drop mine.

Mrs. Mulvenny moved off with a whirr toward her filing cabinets. She hauled open a drawer, dug inside, and pulled out a rolled-up map.

"Let's see," she said, coming around to our side and unrolling it on her table. "Ah yes," she muttered, peering closely at it through her spectacles. "Swans' Nesting, you mean. There were swans then."

"They say they found a tunnel," said Jenny.

"Of course they did. My husband built it. It's all in my book, *Loon Lake Madness*."

I moved up alongside her. "The book's missing from the library. Someone stole it."

Mrs. Mulvenny tapped on the footrest of her wheelchair with tiny black shoes. "Don't have another. It was such a good seller." She paused, then added. "That's a joke boy. Get it?" She drove back to the file cabinet and replaced the map. "Now my husband was a great man," she said, "but a product of his times. You've heard of the Roaring Twenties, haven't you? They do teach history still, don't they?

We nodded. I didn't tell her about Dad and his book.

"We were all mad then. We believed that thinking about something was the same as doing it. We built this crazy house over five years by just adding things on as the fancy took us."

"And the tunnel?" said Jenny gently.

"Well, my husband started to build a tunnel from Swans' Nesting north to the Salmon River in Quebec. He was going to build a canal from the Salmon to the Connecticut River and out into the Atlantic. Crazy it was. I mean who would . . . ?"

She stopped. "See that picture?"

We looked. Beneath a black covering, I saw the Egyptians building pyramids.

"My husband's the man dressed like a pharoah and that's the tunnel."

She was right; it wasn't a pyramid after all.

"Now I've just remembered a business trip I made in 1939. I must examine my tax return."

"But what happened," I said, as we rose to go. "To the tunnel?"

"The tunnel was cut under the mountain for about five miles. Maybe a couple of miles of canal were dug in Canada. Then came the Crash and the Depression. We lost everything except this silly house we'd built as a joke."

She tipped the contents of a box marked "1939" onto the table. "Then one day, Frank went to Swans' Nesting and drowned himself. It broke his heart to be poor and helpless, you see." She began putting papers into piles, then I realized she was crying very softly. Jenny gave me a nod, and we tiptoed from the room.

We almost tripped over Bickerstaffe who'd obviously had his ear to the keyhole. He straightened up real quickly and pretended to be tying his shoelaces.

He showed us out of a side door shaped like a porthole. "Don't you kids come back, not ever. Mrs. Mulvenny needs her rest. Now 'oppit!"

We hopped it.

"Boy, that's a weird old lady," said Jenny. "I thought she might fall apart there and then."

"She very unhappy," said Nguyen. "I bet Mr. Bicker-staffe stole her book and sold it."

When we reached the gate, I looked back. The butler was standing by the house still watching us.

"I wonder what he's trying to hide?" said Jenny.

"Why should he be trying to hide anything?" I asked, sliding through the gate.

"Well, for one thing he wears scent."

"You mean cologne," I said, steadying the bike while she got on.

"I mean scent. Cheap stuff."

Trust a girl to notice that kind of thing. But it did seem a bit odd now she mentioned it.

5

Midnight at the Swamp

Jenny came back with us to the cabin. Dad grinned, shook her hand and said something about the picture on her T-shirt. Then he went back to his word processor. Since he forgot it was lunchtime, we fixed our own. About four Jenny left because she had a babysitting job. She borrowed my bike.

That night we turned in early; I was asleep as soon as my head touched the pillow, but around midnight I woke up. Someone was outside the cabin. I could hear noises in the dark. Little noises, but plain enough.

I rolled over, swung my feet out of bed and shook Nguyen's shoulder.

"Wake up," I whispered, "there's someone outside."

Both of us held our breath and listened.

"Must be Bandit."

"No," I whispered, "he wouldn't make a racket like that."

We crept into the main room and stood behind the drapes of the picture window. Someone or something was on the deck outside.

It was dark in the cabin with the drapes closed, but there was enough light for me to see Nguyen. I couldn't speak without the person outside hearing, but I pointed to the light switch by the door. Then I reached over and took my aluminum baseball bat from its box near the door.

There was a rattling sound on the doorknob. Jeez! Then I realized we hadn't locked it. No one ever locks doors in Scottsville, which is real dumb.

The door stuck for a second then opened. A shadowy figure stood outside.

"Now," I shouted. Nguyen switched on the lights. The figure screamed—just in time.

"It's Jenny," yelled Nguyen.

I lowered the baseball bat.

"Keep your fur on," she hissed. "I'm not Jack the Ripper."

"What do you mean sneaking up here in the middle of the night," I demanded. "You nearly scared me to death."

"You didn't do so bad with me either," she admitted, flopping on the sofa.

She had a new T-shirt with a woman climbing a telephone pole on it. It read "Never underestimate the power of a woman."

"I want to see the tunnel," Jenny said. "I couldn't get away until my parents went to bed." She got up and wandered around the cabin poking into things.

"You could have phoned," I said. "And why do we have to go now? We can go tomorrow. You nearly got flattened with a baseball bat creeping around like that."

"I can't wait 'til tomorrow. I strike while the iron's hot. And I wasn't creeping around," she continued, "I was trying not to advertise my presence, and . . . and . . ."

"Well?"

"I couldn't find the door. And another thing, you guys might have given me a heart attack. Think what a loss that would be to medical science."

"We've not going to that tunnel, now or ever again," I said.

Nguyen backed me up. "No way," he said nodding. "No way."

"OK, OK," said Jenny. "I'll wait 'til tomorrow and ask your dad about it. I expect he knows you went out there."

That's all we needed right now—blackmail.

Leaving us to think that over, Jenny went outside and came back with a dark blue backpack. She emptied it on the floor. "We've got to have candles."

"Don't see why," I said, still mad at her for the

scare she'd given us. "You've brought a pocket flash-light."

She picked up the two large white candles. "Shows what you know. These things are not only good for lighting, they also act as a test of the air."

"How?"

"If the air's bad, the flames dies down and maybe goes out. If there's a gas around, the flames change color, and then boy look out."

"Where'd you hear all this?"

"I told you, I'm going to be a scientist. In the old days miners took canaries underground. If the canary died, the miners got out fast."

Neither Nguyen or I said anything. I thought I remembered hearing something like that somewhere.

"And this little flashlight," she went on, "is for emergencies. You slip it in your back pocket and forget about it."

Also lying on the floor were three Classic Cokes and several bags of potato chips. As usual everyone wanted the green onion flavor, and no one wanted the barbecue. And the colas were warm.

"All I want to do is take a look," Jenny said between crunches. "I mean, is that asking too much?"

I thought it was, but there didn't seem to be any way out of it. For one thing, no one would be able to sleep after all the ruckus, and, for another, Jenny wouldn't leave until she got her way.

We left, still chomping on the potato chips. The moon was round and full, and where the trees hung over the path, the road was shadowed with patterns of silver and black. Sounds of small animals and insects filled the air around us.

The three of us walked along Indian fashion—Jenny in the middle, me in the lead. No one spoke.

The path under the cliff face was pretty narrow even in daylight. I had the flashlight but it wasn't much help. Something salty trickled down the side of my nose. I was sweating.

It was a relief to make it to the boathouse. Nguyen and I dragged the canoe out and pushed it into the Swamp.

The water looked cold and uninviting. A slight night breeze ruffled the water and made tiny white waves that lapped against the shore.

"It's going to be pretty cramped in the canoe," I said, keeping my voice down, the way you do at night. "Jenny, you go in the middle."

For once she didn't argue. We paddled as quietly as possible. It wasn't difficult to see, but once among the reeds and islands it sure was hard to find our way around. It was like a maze. Narrow channels crisscrossed, and since we couldn't see above the reeds, it was impossible to know which direction we were heading.

"Not lost, are you?" said Jenny.

"No." I replied. "We're heading north . . . I think."

"I've got a compass." She must have dug it out of her jeans' pocket. The canoe rocked a little.

Then we followed her directions. Lots of "starboard here," "port here," stuff. At one time, when we passed a reed bed, there was a slithering sound and a plop as a water snake took off. There was a startled sound from Jenny. Her voice got a little shaky for a while.

It was Nguyen who found the channel. The compass was useful in getting us in the right direction. After that he took over paddling, away in the stern and brought us right to the narrow channel to the tunnel.

"Great work, Nguyen," said Jenny.

"There they are," I said, "the ferns."

I felt Jenny lean forward; she rested her head on my shoulder. "You sure? I don't see any way in."

I ignored her. The ferns parted like a green curtain. Seconds later we were inside.

"Phew," said Jenny. "Great smell."

It was cold too, and I shivered even though I was wearing a thick T-shirt.

When Nguyen turned on the flashlight, it scarcely penetrated the blackness ahead. For a moment, it looked like we were going to ram a solid wall. Then he swung the beam to the sides.

"It's big," said Jenny. "Much bigger than I expected." Her voice echoed down the tunnel.

We paddled slowly until Nguyen's flashlight picked

out the iron gate. "That's as far as we can go, Jenny," I said.

"I want to look. Closer."

The canoe bumped against the bars. There was a dull thud that bounced all around us.

"That's it."

Jenny crawled down the canoe, pushing me right into the bow. She leaned over and felt in the water. "There's something here," she whispered excitedly. "It's cold and . . . and . . . shaped like a bolt."

Jenny was breathing heavily, then there was a screeching sound that set my teeth on edge. "Push now," she said.

The gate moved a few inches, but no further. I pushed against it, making the boat lurch in the water. It moved away as I pushed, and I had to let go of the gate. Water was slapping noisily against the side of the tunnel and the canoe.

"You two paddle," I said, "I'll push."

Finally we got the gate far enough open to let the canoe slide by. The rest of the tunnel, as far as we could tell from the flashlight, was as inviting as a barrel of slime.

"Well, we've come this far," I said, with a confidence I didn't feel. "Let's see what's up there."

We paddled for ages. Nothing changed except the tunnel got darker and smelled worse, if possible. In the dim light, I could make out what appeared to be a ledge on the left, just above the water line. In several places it had broken off. It was very dark, and after all Jenny's big deal about poison gas we couldn't light the candles because we all had to help with the boat. The air sure smelled bad enough to kill a canary or two.

"I'll bet we're under Canada now," said Jenny. "I figure we've gone about three miles."

"If we have," I said, "the tunnel will end pretty soon. Remember, Mrs. Mulvenny said only five miles were dug from this side of the border."

When we finally hit the end of the tunnel, it was such a shock that we all tumbled into the bottom of the boat. We were lucky not to lose a paddle. I'd hate to be five miles underground looking for a paddle.

It was a big anticlimax, though I didn't know what I'd expected. It was just five miles of tunnel ending in an earthern wall. We'd all smell like sewer rats for days.

"You'll need your dad's cologne," said Jenny. "Phew it's awful. Wonder how deep it is?"

I stuck my paddle over the side, leaning over until it touched bottom. "Hardly four feet," I muttered.

"Let's get out of here," she said, and no one argued.

We locked the metal gate on the way out; Jenny insisted on that.

The moon was bright and the tall grass and reeds were almost whistling in the light breeze. We paddled quietly through the maze. When suddenly Jenny grabbed my arm. I sucked in my breath; I'd heard it too. Men's voices; one of them very familiar.

"I tell you, they ain't here."

"And I tell you, Isaac, that there was a canoe out here. I saw it from the cliff. That's why I got you."

A small trolling engine sounded nearby. "Well, they ain't 'ere now." It was Bickerstaffe. "And I want to get back. You can never predict what that crazy woman will do next."

The engine sound drew closer. The boat was separated from us by a small island of tall grasses. Very gently I eased my paddle into the water and began pulling us in the direction of a narrow gap in the reeds. Nguyen also paddled. Without a sound, we slid into a covering of wet, floppy reeds—out of sight, and just in time.

The other boat came around the island, not ten feet from us.

"Go over to the right," said Bickerstaffe. "And take it easy." Looking directly at us he said, "Over there, towards them reeds."

I just knew they could hear the pounding of my heart. They couldn't miss us now. One more yard and they'd be on top of us. I prayed Jenny and Nguyen wouldn't move.

The trolling motor was on idle. I couldn't make out much of the other man, Bickerstaffe's body blocked him.

"I'm not going in those reeds," came the reply in a flat, menacing tone. "They'll foul the propeller, and I'd hate to think of your rowing us home."

The engine engaged, and the boat slowly backed away. "And, Isaac, I hope you've made plans to recover that item you so carelessly dropped overboard last week. The Consortium was very displeased. Very displeased."

"It was an accident," whined Bickerstaffe.

"Be careful *you* don't have one," said the other man. "I've grown fond of you, Isaac. I'd miss you."

We could hardly believe it. Again, I felt myself giving an involuntary shudder. As Bickerstaffe and the other man moved slowly away into the darkness.

"That a mighty close haircut," muttered Nguyen.

"Shave," I corrected him. "A mighty close shave."

"I wasn't a bit scared," said Miss You-know-who.

6

The Ruined Farmhouse

The next morning Dad was in a rare mood. The word processor blew a fuse, and he had to take it to Colebrook. It didn't help when the guy in the store charged him fifty cents for a part and twenty-five bucks to put it in.

At lunchtime Jenny arrived on my bike carrying her bag. I was sort of surprised to see her. When I heard what she had in mind, I about blew a fuse myself.

"You want to do what?" I said. "You're crazy."

"Keep your fur on. All I want to do is go into Quebec and find the canal on the Canadian side."

I couldn't believe it. "After what you heard last night," I said. "All that stuff about accidents."

"That was Bickerstaffe."

She looked at me; I looked right back.

"I could ask your dad, of course," she said. "He'll probably . . ."

"All right, all right," I said. "You made your point." Jeez!

Dad didn't look up when I told him we were going on a hike. "Watch out for sharks in the lake," he added, eyes fixed on the word processor's screen.

I hoped the Emperor Titus was worth it.

We used the rowboat this trip; the canoe was a bit small, and we had to have life jackets on.

It was past noon when we reached the far side of Loon Lake; we didn't go into the Swamp but landed just below the neck of water that leads to it. Then we moved up the hill and headed north.

We made pretty good progress at first; it wasn't that steep, and we climbed up a gully toward the tree line. There were lots of ferns and juniper and broken-off chunks of rock. Nguyen was humming to himself while Jenny and I were puffing. The hill was blazing hot; there wasn't any shade below the tree line. The view of Loon Lake was terrific from up there, and the sky was light blue with not a cloud in sight.

Jenny gave me a shove. "No time for sightseeing," she said. "Let's get into the shade."

Sweat was gathering on my neck causing a prickling sensation. Boy, I hate that. If you rub it, the skin feels raw, but you almost can't leave it alone.

Occasionally sounds would carry from the lake, but mostly we heard the steady drone of insects. It was too hot for mosquitoes, but I didn't want to bet they wouldn't be in the trees.

"Let's stop and eat," I said, as we reached the shelter of the fir tree.

Jenny was as glad as I was; she dropped down next to me. Nguyen stood looking back at the lake.

High above, a red-tailed hawk wheeled and dived into the Swamp.

"Scratch one chipmunk," said Jenny.

I couldn't tell if she was right, but the bird had something in its talons when it rose and flew off to the west.

Jenny dug in her bag and took out three cans of Coke. Warm as usual. She had a submarine sandwich cut in three and three Hostess fruit pies. Mine was the lemon one which was OK. She'd also packed three paper plates and napkins with a frilly blue and pink pattern on it. There was even a small white bag for the trash.

We ate mainly in silence watching the birds flying above Loon Lake and the Swamp. There was no wind and a flight of swifts darted above the water. The hawk returned and soared above, solitary but menacing.

Jenny collected all the scraps, stuffed them into the bag and fastened her backpack.

"Let's go," she said, leading us back into the trees.

It was much cooler in the wood. We all shivered a bit until we got used to it. The mosquitoes weren't too bad, which was something.

"Don't swat them," said Jenny, "it only attracts their attention."

The path soon dwindled to nothing, and we had to step through thick undergrowth.

"We've got to go more northeast," I said, "We've gone too much to the west."

We walked for a long time. At first we talked—at least Jenny and I did. Then we stopped because it was too much effort. The forest was quite still, though the occasional squirrel skittered by.

It was hard to pinpoint the exact time when I began to suspect someone was following us. I didn't say anything because the imagination plays tricks in the woods, especially when you're in a dark area. But human sounds just sound different from animal. You can tell.

We were walking single file along a deer path. On each side were thick woods. Mostly they were fir trees. Sometimes a rabbit would jump up right underfoot; they always wait till the last second.

"I wonder how far we've come?" said Jenny. "Feels like miles."

"Well—we are going downhill," I said. "If there's a canal, it's probably down there at the bottom of the slope."

The Ruined Farmhouse

We passed a fallen tree; at the far end was a big red squirrel. He was examining a berry, lifting it in his paws, sniffing and looking at us, all at the same time. He drew his incisors across its surface. Then, as if disgusted, he threw it aside, turned on his perch, shook his tail at us and vanished into the gloom.

"He mighty picky," said Nguyen.

We all laughed.

The trees got thicker, and the darkness closed around us. And boy was it quiet. I knew the others could hear my heart thumping. There wasn't any wind and the leaves didn't stir.

Suddenly something was tugging at my arm. I probably jumped three feet straight into the air.

"Keep your fur on," said Jenny.

"Jeez. Don't do that," I said. "It's scary enough without you grabbing me."

"Oh, come on. Boy, are you dumb!"

She led the way along a narrow path and then, without warning, we stumbled on a clearing along the trees ahead of us. In the middle of it were two buildings—an old wooden farmhouse and a barn—hiding among the trees. They seemed out of place, like someone had just picked them up and dumped them in the middle of nowhere. It was deserted. Trees and bushes were pressing up against the house and smothering it with green creepers that had crawled up the far wall and wrapped themselves around the chimney, which stuck up like a broken tooth because the brickwork had collapsed on one side.

I shuddered though I didn't know why and looked around quickly to see if Jenny had noticed.

"It sure rumbledown," said Nguyen.

"Tumbledown," I muttered, but he didn't hear.

There was a high, peaked roof, most of which had been blown away, leaving gaping holes and long dangling strips of roof tiles. The beams stood out like bones.

Nearby was a small barn, and it was in even worse shape. The roof had sagged in the middle and had collapsed at one end. The door had lost its hinge at the top, so it was leaning forward ready to fall the minute the hinge at the bottom gave way.

"Keep away from that door," I said. "It's going any minute."

"Only the ivy hold this place together," said Nguyen pulling on a piece.

A whole piece about thirty feet long fell around him.

"Very clever," snorted Jenny "and if you'd been right the whole barn would be on top of us. What's inside?"

I circled the barn until I found a window. The glass was real dirty, but I could see enough to know the place wasn't used much. On the far side of the barn was a big bundle of flattened cardboard boxes. Hanging from the walls were pieces of leather harness and some lengths of rope with dusty cobwebs spun between them.

"Well?" demanded Jenny.

"Crushed carboard boxes, some old rusty tools. There's an old workbench covered in dust . . ."

"What kind of tools?"

"An old rusty saw with a red handle, a pair of pliers . . ."

"OK. OK, let's check the house out."

Now that was just like Jenny Weber. She was forever sticking her nose into someone else's business. "What if the owner catches us," I said.

"Owner! What owner? This place's a wreck."

"There's a sign," said Nguyen. "Say 'No Trespassers' and 'Posted No Hunting'. What it mean?"

"It means," Jenny replied. " 'Keep out' and," she paused before adding quietly, "whoever put up the sign really means it." The woods around us were somehow quieter and more threatening. It was colder and there was a damp wood smell.

A driveway of sorts led up to the house from the far side. It was overgrown with grass and weeds and wild roses.

"What a dump," said Jenny. "Hasn't been lived in for years."

I bent down in the driveway. "Then what about these tire tracks in the mud here," I said, pointing.

She knelt beside me. "They're fresh," Jenny said. "Someone's been here in the last few days. I wonder why?"

I got up and looked around quickly. A shadow moved among the trees. Suddenly I shivered again, and it wasn't from the cold.

"This place real spooky," said Nguyen.

"You said it," I replied. "You said it."

7

Trapped

Of course I knew what was going to happen. When common sense said "let's go," Jenny Weber was saying, "let's look around inside."

"What for?" I asked, a bit too quickly. "I mean we were looking for the canal weren't we?"

"Oh come on," she said, "let's check it out. We'll never find that old canal anyway."

"It's got to be near," I insisted. "We've come about five miles."

She wasn't listening but was walking up to the rickety old porch.

"We go too?" asked Nguyen.

"No, we don't. She won't get far. All the windows

are boarded up, and the doors will be locked solid. This is going to be sweet."

Jenny crossed the porch and tried the door. Sure enough it didn't budge. "It's locked," I whispered to Nguyen. "Told you."

Jenny put a brave face on it; she wouldn't look at us. Instead she started wandering around looking between the rotting wooden planks of the porch. Then she knelt down and stuck her arm between two broken boards. She grunted, got lower until she was lying flat on the porch and fished around with her hand. Finally she carefully withdrew her hand. There was an old rusty beer can.

"She flipped her cover," muttered Nguyen.

"Lid," I corrected him automatically.

Jenny left the porch and looked around until she found an old brick and a rock. Putting the can on the brick, she hammered away with the rock until the can was flatter than a flitter.

I was determined not to ask what she was doing. I'd have died first. When Nguyen was about to speak, I shook my head.

Jenny took the flat piece of can back to the door and slid it between the lock and the door. Nguyen and I took a few steps forward without even knowing it. She wiggled the tin up and down, listened carefully, then turned the knob and pushed. The door opened.

"Could have done it in half the time," she said grinning, "if I'd had a credit card."

"Where'd you learn to do that?" I demanded.

She grinned, showing her braces. "It's on every cop show on TV. Everyone knows that."

I didn't, but I sure wasn't going to admit it.

Jenny wiped her hands on her jeans and skimmed the can into the bushes. "Come on, you two, not scared are you?"

That got me on the porch, it creaked like mad. Already it smelled musty and damp.

"Wonder who lived here?" Jenny asked. "Crazy place to build a farm."

Nguyen was picking his way carefully across the porch; the boards groaned then, with a crack like a rifle shot, his foot went through. "This place ready to fall down," he said, pulling up the leg of his jeans and looking at the place on his leg where the skin had been taken off.

"Does it hurt?" asked Jenny.

"It OK."

"Well, come on then."

Jenny pushed the door wide open and stepped inside. "I just want to take a quick peek."

"Hope no one live here with big dog," said Nguyen still rubbing his leg. "Dog bite finish this leg off."

"Oh, stop going on about—Will you look at the wallpaper! Pink cupids." She tore a strip off; it unpeeled from floor to ceiling in one long roll. The plaster behind was brown. I touched it, and it was soaked.

The dining room still had a rusty brass chandelier hanging from the ceiling. I guess brass can be rusty. Anyway, it was sort of greenish. And there was junk piled everywhere—porcelain wash basins, a couple of awful old jugs with sunflowers carved on the sides, and three metal buckets in the kitchen sink all with the bottoms rusted out.

The place had been used recently. There were cigarette butts and empty beer cans on the floor.

"What this?" asked Nguyen, picking up an old-fashioned coffee grinder.

"You grind up coffee beans in it," I explained. "Gramps still uses his in Michigan." I felt a bit strange after I'd said this because my Gramps was now Nguyen's Gramps—though they'd never met.

Jenny was playing scientist, probing and prodding. "This is the water pump," she said from the kitchen. There was a loud clanking noise. When I got to the kitchen it was just in time to see a tiny trickle of rusty brown water drip from the iron spout.

"Still works."

"If you call that working," I said.

Each window on the ground floor had heavy boards nailed over it. The only light came from between the boards and from a hole in the ceiling. I could see right through it and through a gap in the roof. The main room must have been the living room because there was a fireplace made of cobblestones—the kind you dig up in your yard. The hearth was filled with old bricks.

"Chimney fall in," said Nguyen. "Wonder why?"

"Raccoons," said Jenny.

This caused a look of amazement on my brother's face.

"They make nests in chimneys and dislodge the old cement," Jenny explained.

"Ah. Now I get it."

"This place is crazy," I said. "Look at all the mattresses."

Under an archway was a smaller room with a long table and lots of broken chairs all piled up and mostly smashed. Against one wall were a dozen mattresses. They'd all been stacked up at one time but now the top ones had slid off.

"Rats eat feathers," said Nguyen pointing to several holes. He reached out to grab a handful.

"They don't *eat* feathers," sniffed Jenny. "Those are probably their nests."

Nguyen drew his hand back quickly.

There was a little bathroom too; the sink was hanging crazily off the wall. When I touched it the whole thing crashed to the floor. The noise would have waked the dead.

"Will you cool it," hissed Jenny. "I wanted to take a look, not flatten the place."

"How was I . . ."

"Sometimes you guys don't have half a brain between you. What if Nguyen got bitten by a rat; and you crushed your foot out here in the back of the beyond? Keep your hands off things."

That Jenny Weber was just about the bossiest kid I ever met. I've had teachers who lectured me less.

"Let's go upstairs," she added.

I drew the line at that. "Not me," I said. "I didn't want to come in here in the first place. Those stairs don't look too . . ."

It didn't faze her; she crossed the room, and started to climb holding on to the banister with one hand.

"The newel post pretty shaky," said Nguyen.

"The what?" Jenny had stopped.

"The newel post," repeated Nguyen.

Jenny looked at me, then him. "Is that Vietnamese or what?"

"The post at the end of the stairs is a newel post," he said. "Right Jeff?"

I didn't have the slightest idea. I'd sure never heard of it, but I nodded and said, "Right."

"There's no such word in English," said Jenny going up the stairs. "If there was I would have heard of it. Of course, if you boys are afraid to risk life and limb stay down there."

64

That did it, of course. Nguyen and I climbed the stairs giving the mattress a good kick as we crawled over it. Tiny brown feathers flew around us. One got up my nose and started me sneezing.

"Typical," said Jenny from one of the bedrooms.

On the second floor there was a lot more light. The roof was just about shot. We couldn't see much because the farmhouse was surrounded by higher ground, and hemmed in by trees. Once again it was pretty obvious no one had been up the stairs in years.

"Three bedrooms and a bathroom," said Jenny. "In about a year, the bathtub will be in the kitchen."

"This must be big family," said Nguyen "like in Vietnam. So far count twelve mattresses."

"That is a bit odd," Jenny said. "But farmers always have big families."

"My uncle Ambrose only has one kid," I informed her. "He told me he didn't have time to get a family. When he wasn't farming, he played golf. Even in the snow he said."

"I didn't mean *every* farmer has a big family. That was a generalization. *Most* farming families . . ."

She broke off. Nguyen and I instinctively crouched. A van was drawing up in front of the farm house. The engine died away. In less than a minute a second vehicle drew up. It was a Jeep with two men in it.

"Keep down," hissed Jenny pulling me to the floor. "You want to get us arrested?"

When the passenger in the car got out, I knew we wouldn't be arrested. You couldn't mistake that accent and the complaining.

"Why do we 'ave to do this now?" Bickerstaffe whined. "It's my day off. You don't know, and Dietz don't know just what it's like to live with that old crazy bat. She had me sort all her receipts for 1940 into fifty-eight different piles. Fifty-eight! Do you know she kept every sales receipt from every store she ever visited. Ere, what's that?"

We watched in horror as tiny feathers floated from a gap in the well downstairs towards the men.

"Jeez," I muttered. "What happened?"

"Air currents," hissed Ms. Know-It-All. "We tore up a mattress, and any slight change in pressure or wind direction will set the feathers off. Lucky for us, or there would be dust everywhere with our footprints in it."

Boy, she said a mouthful. A regular stream of brown moldy feathers was drifting through the air. The man with Bickerstaffe moved towards the house. His face reminded me of a weasel—small sharp eyes and a mean look. His hand went inside his coat and came out with a gun.

Jenny made a gurgling sound; Nguyen had gone pale; I'm sure I was too.

"Now wait a bit," said Bickerstaffe taking a step back at the sight of the gun. "What's up? Them's just feathers."

"Check the door." The voice was flat and nasal.

"Bet he's from New York," whispered Jenny. "Probably Brooklyn."

I could have killed her!

All three of us froze where we were. Bickerstaffe stepped onto the porch. Apparently he knew just where to put his feet. If he hadn't, every one of the rotten planks would have snapped.

"Well?"

"One of these 'ere boards is broke."

The other man joined him. "And the door?"

"Locked."

If I'd looked at Jenny I knew she would be totally smug. The way she got in hadn't damaged the lock, so the door had closed behind us.

"Take a look inside," said nasal voice.

"Now look Mr. Vadillo," said Bickerstaffe. "Anything could have broken this wood . . . a deer—"

"An antelope, Rudolph the red-nosed reindeer . . . get in Bickerstaffe. You're in enough trouble as it is."

A key wiggled in the lock; we could hear it. Then the door opened. That was all Jenny needed. "Come on," she said, "and quick."

She led the way into the far bedroom. It was the smallest one, but it had a large closet with three mattresses in it. In seconds, we were jammed inside, with the door closed probably long before the English butler had got into the farmhouse.

In the distance, we could hear voices, but I couldn't make out the words. Neither could Jenny so she opened the door a bit. Jeez!

"Just split, that's all, and the feathers blew out."

"Check it out," said Vadillo in the same flat threatening tone he always used.

"Now I ain't climbing those stairs. Let Maddox do it."

"Am I to tell Mr. Johnson or Deitz you've been troublesome again. He's a man who doesn't have my sense of humor. Now get up there."

With much grumbling and puffing, the butler began his ascent. Seconds later there was a loud crash and several cuss words from Bickerstaffe that I heard when a publisher rejected one of Dad's books. There was more banging and finally a tremendous crash followed by a howl from the butler.

"I've broke my bleedin' back. I 'ope you're satisfied. The newel post collapsed . . ."

Jenny seemed to have stopped breathing, and in the darkness I swear I could see a huge grin on Nguyen's face.

"And now there's no way up with all them stairs gone."

"All right, all right. I'll go. Have Maddox look around outside and in the basement. He's too comfortable in that van. He should have been here hours ago guarding the place. He's never around when you want him. And you watch the stairs."

There was more climbing, some grunts, and then the unmistakable sound of footsteps coming along the top landing. Jenny eased the door shut.

"See anything," said Bickerstaffe from below. He sounded much closer than before, but I guess you hear better when you're in real danger.

"I don't see anything . . ."

There was a sudden loud explosion. For a moment, I thought it was the gun. It wasn't, Vadillo had begun sneezing. And once he started he couldn't stop.

"He's allergic to the feathers," Jenny hissed. "Oh boy!"

It seemed forever before Vadillo could stop. When he did he said. "We ought to burn these damn mattresses, take them all out. I've half a mind to . . ."

Jenny grabbed my arm and squeezed. Boy, if Vadillo started looking for mattresses we'd be done for.

"You coming down then?"

"In a minute; there's some closets and the bathroom yet. There's evidence of something coming up here. Probably those damn raccoons. Or maybe your reindeer, Isaac." He gave an evil laugh."

We heard him banging around in the bathroom.

"Get under the mattresses," whispered Jenny; "it's our only hope."

The one thing about those mattresses was they didn't make any noise. Well, moving them sounded like the end of the world to us in the closet, but Vadillo was banging around in the bathroom so he didn't hear anything.

The three of us were piled right on top of each other now. If we'd been jammed before, now we were squashed. I could hear Jenny's heart and feel Nguyen's breath on my cheek. My head was flattened against a wall, and I could feel the vibrations of Vadillo's shoes on the floor outside. He came right along the hall and into the bedroom.

"For once Bickerstaffe you might be right," he shouted. "There's no one here."

The closet door was suddenly yanked open. We were less than a foot from a man with a loaded gun.

"More damn mattresses," he muttered. He sneezed several times. "Damn them. I think," he raised his voice so the butler could hear. "Nothing but moldy mattresses. I think I'll just shoot some holes in these."

8

Descent

The three of us had all stopped breathing. I could see Vadillo, smiling for once, about to pull the trigger and explode three mattresses. The very same mattresses we were hidden behind.

"Better not," shouted Bickerstaffe. "Them feathers will start you off agin."

There was a click, not loud.

"That's about the only sensible thing I've ever heard you say." Vadillo replied, his voice already moving away from us.

Right at that moment, just when everything was going right, I felt this sneeze coming on. It was the craziest thing. When everything looked as if it was going to be OK, I had a chance to blow it.

In the distance, I heard Vadillo climbing downstairs. There was more cursing and banging. At that moment, I covered my face with my hand and let out a stream of sneezes one after the other. The other two, horrified, tried to help, but it was Nguyen who found the solution. He pushed my face down into one of the mattresses.

The door below slammed shut.

"Fine thing," said Jenny when all was clear. "You nearly got us shot to pieces."

"Whose idea was it to come in here in the first place?" I demanded. "I didn't want to come, did I?"

Nguyen looked from one to the other of us. He was smart enough to change the subject. "Let's go," he said.

We climbed down the stairs. Jenny was the last. As she passed the torn mattress, she couldn't resist one final attack on it.

"Feather volcano," said Jenny, jerking the mattress which disintegrated and feathers exploded everywhere.

We all flapped, and I sneezed, but finally the feathers settled on their own.

"Let's get out of here," I said, peeping out through a gap in the boarded up window. One look was enough. The jeep had gone, but the van was still there. It had Canadian plates and was close enough for me to read them.

Jenny was reaching for the front door knob.

"Wait," I cautioned her, they're still here."

She looked startled for a minute then moved over to where I stood and looked intently at the van. "Looks empty," she murmured uneasily.

"You want to risk getting shot with Vadillo's six gun," I whispered. "He's longing for a chance to kill something with it."

"It was an automatic, not a revolver."

"So what, a bullet's a bullet."

"Right. And if we try to prize the boards off the windows at the back, he's bound to catch on."

Jenny crept back to the door and turned the handle; the door moved a fraction then stuck. "Oh boy," she said. "I think they put a padlock on it. We're trapped, and it's all my fault." She sat on the edge of a mattress pulling up her knees and resting her head on them.

Jeez, that was clever! I was going to remind her that she was the one who wanted to explore the farmhouse. Now I couldn't without feeling like a jerk.

At last I said, "We have to do something. If Dad realizes we're gone, he'll blow his stack."

"Will have lake dragged for bodies," added Nguyen.

"To say nothing of the lecture we'll get. 'How worried he was,' 'how when we have kids we'll see just how worried parents get.' We've got to get out of here."

Jenny was looking at some feathers floating near her. She blew at them; they flipped upside down, moving rapidly away, then settling down.

"What makes them move about?" she asked no one in particular.

"You said air currents."

See that was just like her. There was a mad killer with a gun trying to blow us away, and Jenny Weber was watching feathers floating about. She got to her feet and began working her way down the passage to the kitchen.

"When I was back here," she said, "there was quite a draft."

"Place nothing but holes," Nguyen commented.

"Right," I added; "the whole house is like Swiss cheese. Didn't you see the angle of the chimney? It'll probably fall through the roof on us."

"This is different. You have lots of holes, and there's no particular current; this was very strong."

Now I got an inkling of what she was talking about. In old houses they had those entrances leading directly into the cellar. If we could find a way out without making a noise, we could maybe sneak off. *If*, and it was a big if, the cellar entrance didn't face the van. Still I sure didn't have a better plan, so I followed Jenny back into the kitchen. She moved slowly around the room pausing now and then. Nguyen and I watched as she circled the room, finally stepping in front of the basement door.

There's a draft coming from in there," she said. "I could feel it on my legs." It opened silently and easily. Beyond was a series of wooden steps leading to a dark basement. The air was cold and damp.

"Let's take a look," she said.

The flashlight helped a little, but at the bottom of the steps it was pitch black.

"I'll go first," Jenny said, "give me the light."

"Be careful," I said handing it to her, "there may be water over the bottom steps."

"Maybe rats, too," added Nguyen.

"You think I'm afraid of rats?" Jenny snorted.

"No. Just me," replied Nguyen.

We heard her stepping from one step to another, the light bobbing as she moved. Once it wobbled wildly; there was a squeaking sound and what seemed to be a stifled scream.

"She find rat," Nguyen whispered to me.

"I heard that," Jenny said from below. "Well, you brave men can join me down here. There's nothing but cardboard packing and tissue paper."

Our eyes adjusted to the light.

"Help me move the cases," said Jenny, handing me one.

"What for? They're only cardboard boxes."

"How old?"

"How should I know."

"Well," she said, "they're not as old as this house, are they?"

We finally moved all forty-one boxes. Nguyen did just what she told him though I think he thought Jenny was nuts.

Every box was either empty or full of green tissue paper. I dug into one box and pulled every scrap of tissue paper from it. "Nothing here," I said.

"Fun-ny!" she answered.

She poked around some more. "What does Olmec mean?" she asked, after a few more bangs.

"Never heard of it," I replied, stuffing tissue into one of the boxes. "Why?"

"It's written on the side of this box in pencil." She held the flashlight. "Someone wrote it down on this box. There's a number too, and a date."

I studied them. "It looks like an 'eight' and 'July seventeenth,'" I said. "Two days from now. What's it mean?"

"Well, that's obvious," she said. You don't have to be Einstein to figure it means eight boxes on July seventeenth."

I hadn't quite worked it out, but I nodded.

"Could be something to do with mechanism," I suggested. "I mean the 'MEC' part."

"The first letter might stand for 'Organization,'" Jenny added.

"Maybe 'Organization of Lazy Mechanics,'" I suggested. "That's what it is; they come here to avoid fixing cars."

"Not funny," she said. "Anyway where's that cold air coming from?" She got down on hands and knees. "Point the flashlight down there."

Within a minute she had taken up four floorboards. They came up easily, and at once we could see that there was a deep dark hole that appeared bottomless. The air was damp as it rushed up at us.

"What's it for," I asked.

Jenny said, "Beats me. Wonder how deep it is?"

"Maybe China," said Nguyen.

"Fun-ny." She shone the light down it.

"Could it be one of those . . . those old toilets?" I suggested. "It sure stinks."

Jenny didn't laugh. "You mean a privy? It's too big. The hole is four feet square, and if you fell down . . ." She giggled. "What a way to go."

Nguyen found a rock that had been dislodged from the stone walls of the cellar.

"Drop it when I say," Jenny told him. "Then everyone count and listen."

We waited. Then she said sharply, "Now."

It fell, and I counted three seconds before there was a splash a long way off. Echoes came banging up the hole immediately after.

Jenny was still kneeling at the edge. "Well, we know there's water down there."

"It really stinks," I said.

"You keep saying that," she replied.

"I counted three seconds," I told her. "Maybe just a bit less. "There's a way to tell how deep it is, isn't there?"

"Of course. Sixteen feet, time squared."

"Time what . . . ?"

"Three seconds squared is nine, nine times sixteen is a hundred forty-four. That hole's about a hundred forty feet deep."

Boy, that was really impressive. She really was a scientist.

"Ah," she said. "Found them."

"Found what?"

"Steps leading down. Hand me the matches and some tissue paper."

I lit a match and stuck it to the edge of the paper. It flared up, almost taking my eyebrows off. I dropped it to the floor.

"Great." Jenny sniffed. "Just great!"

The second time, I took more tissue paper and rolled it into a spill. An updraft scattered tiny red flares around us. For a brief moment, we caught a glimpse of metal steps leading down. The paper was burned up in seconds, but not before I'd been left with the impression of a deep dark hole sinking down to nowhere. The hair was standing up on the back of my neck.

"That one deep hole," said Nguyen in awe. "Maybe go to the center of the earth."

There was a loud sniff from you-know-who.

"I'm going down," Jenny said. "Give me the flashlight."

"Well, I'm not," I retorted. "You don't know where it goes."

"I know it goes down," she said, swinging herself over the edge. "Here I go."

I didn't know what to do. She must have known I was talking sense, but she just ignored me. Her voice echoed up. "Steps all the way. It's easy."

I held out as long as I could, but the sound of her movements got more and more muffled and distant.

"We go too?" asked Nguyen.

"We do not," I answered firmly.

I was bluffing, of course, hoping Jenny would come up. She didn't. And so finally I swung my leg over feeling for the top rung. Nguyen tore stips of cardboard from the packing cases.

"We burn them down there, gives light. Burn more slowly too."

I thought it was a smart idea; I should have thought of it.

The passage was wide enough to be comfortable, but the rungs were greasy, and, boy, did I hang on to them. Nguyen was going to find it tough with the cardboard in one hand.

Below there were sounds from Jenny; they echoed up from a long way below. The air draft was dank and clammy. I read somewhere that coal miners used ladders before they got cages. Those guys sure must have had strong arms. My legs were aching, but my arms felt like they were coming out of their sockets.

With my feet I felt for the next rung, then lowered

myself when I found it. Twice Nguyen trod on my hands with his feet. Each time I heard a distorted "Sorry."

As I went further down, it got darker and darker. Very occasionally there was a glimpse of a bobbing light below. Jenny had the flashlight on, and I guessed sometimes it pointed upwards as she changed her hold on the rungs. Even she wouldn't be holding it between her teeth the way they do in movies.

I was sweating which was crazy because the hole was damp and cold air was rushing up past me. My hands were frozen stiff but there was perspiration running down my back! The whole deal was crazy anyway—three kids going underground without the slightest idea where they'd end up. One thing was for sure. If I lived to tell about it, I sure wouldn't be telling Dad.

Probably I was on the ladder for five minutes before I heard Jenny's voice. It was almost normal.

"I'm down. The water's only three feet deep."

The smell wasn't that bad. Probably I was getting used to it. I took my matches out of my pocket and held them above my head. Jenny's hands guided me down the last few rungs.

Moving out into the water to give Nguyen room, I struck a match. The sudden illumination allowed one quick impression of our surroundings; then the match burned slowly but with little intensity.

One look was enough though. We were standing at the end of a tunnel carved from rock and earth. From the cracks in the rocks a few fungi were growing—all a sort of pale pinkish color. When I touched a fat mushroom it crumpled up into a thousand squishy pieces.

"Probably poisonous," said Jenny, her voice echoing around the end of the tunnel.

I ignored her. The flame had quickly died out. There was a splash and a thud as Nguyen finished his descent and stood in the water up to his waist. Boy, was it cold!

"We back in Mr. Mulvenny's tunnel," he said. "But no canoe."

He was right. I'd seen it at once. The rungs were in the side of the wall some yards from the end of the tunnel, so we hadn't spotted them on our last trip.

"Well, come on," said Jenny; "we can't stay here all day."

"Just a minute," I said; "let's think about this."

"What's to think about," demanded a voice in the darkness. "You want to go back and get a hole drilled in you?"

"It awful dark and cold down here," Nguyen said from the other side of me. Maybe this water get deeper."

"That's right," I added, "just because it's up to our chests doesn't mean it won't get a lot deeper."

"Well . . . you may have a point," Jenny admitted. "Light another piece of cardboard and let's look around."

It wasn't easy. It took a while for the cardboard to catch. One match was wasted because by the time I'd found out where my brother was and got to the cardboard, it had burned out. As it was, I burned my finger, let out a yell and dropped the match. It fizzed in the water.

"Oh, come on. You know there was a ledge along the left wall when we came in before. It's got to be over on the right somewhere."

The next one worked—just. We knew roughly where the cardboard and match would be so Nguyen was ready the minute the match flared.

Even with the increased light, we could see nothing but a long dark passage going straight ahead. The walls were smooth, and the ceiling had been bricked over in some parts not in others. The water was black and uninviting, and there was no way to tell if it would get deeper.

"Look over there," said Jenny squeezing my arm. "All along the right tunnel wall."

About ten yards ahead of us was a narrow ledge running as far as we could see. It was about a foot above the water level.

"It the goatwalk," said Nguyen. "Ouch!"

There was a brief flare of falling cardboard and a fizzing sound. "Burn finger," he added unnecessarily.

I was nearest to the catwalk so I pushed my way toward it holding the matches above my head.

"You on the *goatwalk* yet?" demanded Jenny.

I pulled myself up; it wasn't easy because I could only use one hand. Even when I got on the ledge, it was slippery as glass. First time I stood up, I slipped and almost fell headfirst into the water. I was on both knees when Jenny said, "Well?"

"Yes."

"Move along then, we haven't got all day."

Jenny pretty soon found out the catwalk was no cakewalk. Just standing up was tough; I had to crouch at the knees just to keep my balance.

It was different from being in a room where the light goes out. When that happens, there's still an impression of what was around—a chair, a table, whatever. In the tunnel, it was weird. Anything we touched could have been any shape. Even as we edged along the ledge, there was no way of telling if we were going straight, up, or down. Without the cardboard flames or the little flashlight, we had only a vague idea of where we were going.

Another thing, and I wouldn't have told the others. It was scary down there. We were trapped in a long, dark tunnel and couldn't get out. A million tons of earth was balanced above us. We were swallowed up like Jonah in the whale.

With me in the lead, and Jenny in the middle, we made our way cautiously just about inch by inch. The trick was to keep our right shoulders pressed close to the side of the tunnel. That way our feet followed the ledge. Trouble was, the tunnel wall wasn't as smooth close up as it looked from a distance. My arm was bruised from top to bottom.

Every so often we'd stop, light a piece of cardboard

and take a look ahead. It was always the same—black, greasy water stretching as far as we could see.

A couple of times, my foot slipped and began to slide off the ledge. There was a bitter taste in my mouth. Jeez! Any false step and we'd have been pitched into the water. Every step became more painful because the cold seemed to be creeping up my legs; I was losing the feeling in them. That was bad because every nerve in our feet was needed to keep our footing.

Jenny had kept the flashlight in her jeans' pocket. She was saving it for an emergency, she said. If we weren't in an emergency I don't know who was.

When I lit the last piece of cardboard, Nguyen said, "this tunnel go on forever."

I was beginning to think he was right; Jenny hadn't said much for a long time. As far as I could remember, she hadn't sniffed in disgust either.

The cardboard flared red and fluttered out of my hand and fell into the water. I took a step forward, my foot found nothing. For a second I was suspended in mid-air, the next I was falling. Down! Down! I hit the water, went to the bottom, and was jammed hard against the rock floor of the tunnel. I hit with a bone-crunching thud. The jarring slammed up my back, rammed into my head. My head spun, and I swallowed a gallon of filthy canal water.

When I rose to the surface coughing and spluttering, silver stars were still spinning before my eyes.

There were voices, far away at first, then one became clear. It was Jenny's frightened voice in the gloomy darkness.

"Jeff! Jeff! What happened?"

Nguyen was also shouting my name and the echoes after a long pause came back in a series of cries finally losing strength.

"I'm OK," I said. "The catwalk ends here."

A tiny ray of light shone out from the ledge. Finally it caught me. I swam towards it. Jenny's hand pulled on mine, but she wasn't any help, and I was afraid she'd be pulled in. For several minutes I hung on to the edge of the catwalk getting my breath back.

"There's no point in getting back on the ledge," I said, treading water. "I've got to find out if it ends here or has collapsed."

"Careful Jeff," said Nguyen. "Water tire you out quick."

That wasn't what worried me. Now the water was so deep, we had to swim. But how far? Nguyen could swim ten miles, but what about Jenny? I'd swum three miles, but that was in daylight in warm water. I started off, but in less than a minute was in trouble. I couldn't see where I was going and the next thing I knew was I'd banged my head on the opposite wall. I let my feet drift slowly down, but I couldn't touch bottom.

"I can't tell where I'm going," I shouted. That was a mistake; the echoes bounced back, and when they shouted back, there was more racket than at a basketball game. I waited until it had died away, then said in a normal tone. "Don't shout. Speak normally."

Jenny said. "What are you going to do?"

"I'm going to swim up the tunnel and see if the catwalk goes any further."

There was a splash, then Nguyen spoke almost in my ear. "I swim. You wait."

This made a lot of sense; he was a much better swimmer. But the point was, he couldn't see any better than I could.

A tiny beam of light suddenly came on and picked up Nguyen immediately. Then the light swung up the tunnel. Jenny had the answer. All Nguyen had to do was follow the light.

"They build tunnels this way with a laser," she said. "It goes straight." I didn't say a word.

Nguyen started off; in seconds he was out of sight, there was scarcely any sound at first and none later. Like I say, he swims like a fish.

I scrambled up onto the ledge; it was drier and a lot warmer which wasn't saying much. So we sat and waited.

After a while, Jenny said in a small voice. "How long do you think he's been gone?"

Looking at my watch, I pressed the light button. Nothing happened. " 'Bout ten minutes," I guessed.

"Seems longer."

Another ten minutes dragged slowly by, then another ten. I was getting real nervous and so cold my teeth were chattering. I actually tried holding my chin and pressing it closed. It didn't help.

Then the flashlight began flickering; I heard Jenny slap it against the palm of her hand. The thin beam again pierced the darkness. Neither of us said anything.

A minute later, it flickered again, went out, flickered rapidly, then quit. A few frantic slaps followed. The thin beam of light again pierced the dark, then it went out for good.

"That's that!" Jenny said very softly.

When I heard this, I went as cold inside as I was outside. I slumped back against the cold tunnel wall and waited.

"Eeee oooo . . . eee ooo!"

An eerie moaning sound filled the tunnel and bounced back from all directions at us, before continuing its journey beyond us.

"Jeez! What's that?" I said, shaking like a leaf.

"E e e e ooo!"

Jenny whispered. "I don't know, but it's getting nearer."

Then almost next to us, a familiar voice shouted. "Hello, hello!"

"It's Nguyen!" I screamed. "Nguyen!"

"You two keep your voices down," shouted Jenny. "Quiet!"

"Couldn't see the light," Nguyen explained suddenly at our feet.

"It went out."

"How much further then?" I asked; "I'm freezing."

"Ledge start again in about half mile. Easy from there to gate. Water soon only three feet deep."

I could feel my heart going a mile a minute; it had to be from relief. I eased myself into the water.

"Follow my voice," Nguyen said, "and I lead us."

I heard Jenny sliding into the water. There was a sharp intake of breath. "Boy," she muttered. "It got cold."

Nguyen started swimming; he sang a song in French, and we followed behind. It was freezing but it's different when you know you're safe.

The song stopped; I let my feet fall. They touched bottom; the water was up to my chin. A hand touched me. "Climb up," said Nguyen. I worked my way up on the catwalk. Jenny followed.

After that it was pretty easy. With my brother in the lead, we felt our way along the wall. The catwalk was a good two feet wide and well above the water level so it wasn't as slippery as the other section. In no time at all it seemed we reached the gate.

I knew by feel where the bolt was so I just slipped into the water and felt for it.

"Well," said Jenny, "what's the prob? Yank the bolt and let's go."

"The problem is," I said standing up slowly, "that

there is no way I can reach the bolt from this side. My arm's not long enough. A grown man could do it, but none of us can."

There was a long silence; finally, Jenny spoke. "You mean . . . ?"

"I mean we're trapped here."

There was a longer silence while that sank in.

"What about climbing out," suggested Nguyen. "Go back, climb ladder."

"Do you think we could go back five miles?" I asked. "It took three hours just to get this far."

Jenny moved over to the grate and felt for the bolt. She fumbled for a long time. "You're right," she admitted at last.

"And if we walked back do you think we could climb all those steps? It just about pulled my arms out going down. Climbing up would be a thousand times tougher. Face it. We're trapped."

Even Jenny was silent now.

9

The Cliff Face

No one said anything after that. We all knew we could never make it back, and if we couldn't get out into Loon Lake there was nothing to do until someone came along. If they did, you could bet Bickerstaffe would be with them. We were caught all right—rats in a trap.

I shivered. At first I hadn't noticed how cold it was; I remembered people died of exposure when they were forced to stay out at night.

There was a loud splash. Jenny screamed.

"What happened," I yelled. "Jenny, you OK? Nguyen?"

"Something bumped against my legs," Jenny said. She sounded real scared. "It was big. Big."

"You feel anything, Nguyen?" There was no answer.

"Nguyen," I shouted again, the name echoed all around me, disappearing up the tunnel.

"He's drowning; I know he is," said Jenny. "He's drowning, and we can't see an inch in front of us."

"How can he drown," I said, trying to reassure myself, "Nguyen swims like a fish, and there's only three feet of water."

"Well, where is he?" she demanded.

There was a loud splash and then, almost in my ear, I heard. "I here."

"Where were you?" I demanded. "You scared me out of my—Wait a minute."

"What is it?" said Jenny, anxiously.

I fumbled for the iron grate and put my hand through it. At once I felt something. "Nguyen! You got through the grate."

"He what?"

"He's on the other side," I said. "Nguyen's on the far side of the grille."

Jenny waded over, bumping into me. She must have felt him too. "You're right. He did get through. But how?"

"Very simple," said Nguyen. "Gate made of iron; water made of water."

"What does that mean?" I demanded.

Jenny splashed around and bumped into me. "I get it," she said excitedly. "The grille just goes about a foot below the waterline."

I knelt down. She was right! There was a full two

foot clearance under it. I heard a splash and a few seconds later Jenny spoke from the other side of the gate. "This water's absolutely putrid. I had to have ten showers after the last trip."

Holding my nose and clamping my mouth closed, I dropped down and pushed my legs under the bars. Seconds later I was scrambling to my feet on the far side.

"We'd better make tracks," I said, when I got my breath. "It's late. And Nguyen?"

"Yes."

"Thanks."

"Right," agreed Jenny. "Thanks."

It took less than five minutes to get to the tunnel entrance. For one thing, after fifty yards the tunnel turned enough to let the light outside penetrate. For another we didn't hang around. We'd been gone a few hours—not long enough for dad to call in the Marines, but long enough.

Funny thing. When we waded out through the ferns, the sun was beating down, and nothing looked any different. I even saw the red-tailed hawk above us.

"We pretty messy," said Nguyen.

That was the understatement of the year. There were dirty black water marks all over our clothes. And I could tell that no skunk would come within a mile of us.

"We can't go back like this," Jenny said. "Let's swim."

So we did. The water in the Swamp wasn't very deep, but every so often there was a pool where we could turn head over heels under the water.

"We're like the Water Babies in the old story," I said. "Boy, if Dad saw us now."

"Let's stop and dry off," said Jenny. "Over there."

Just ahead was a large flat island surrounded by a fringe of tall brown grass. Inside was a flat sandy center.

"You guys turn your backs," ordered Jenny. "I want to wring out my shirt."

As if we wanted to look. We turned around anyway; it wasn't worth the hassle.

Drying off didn't take long in the sun. "What about the rowboat?" asked Jenny.

"Let's not fool with it," I replied. "We've only got a mile to go to the boathouse. Nguyen and I will get it later."

We crashed through the reeds into a shallow channel and waded toward the shore. A covey of ducks sprang up in front of us and flew off complaining toward Loon Lake. We were so close I could see all the pinfeathers on one of them.

We didn't stop at the boathouse but took the path to the back cabin. We looked almost normal by now. Jenny took the rubber band from her pony tail and shook her head.

"Does it look clean?"

"Does to me," I replied. "But you can take a shower in the back cabin when we get up there."

"I will," she said. "Maybe several."

I took the lead for the steep, narrow part along the side of the cliff. Out of the corner of my eye, I caught a movement on top of the cliff. I stopped and Jenny pulled up short. "What is it?"

"Nothing," I said. "Thought I saw something."

We went on being careful where we put our feet. Maybe I was more on my guard, at least subconsciously, because when a couple of small rocks fell from above, I looked up again.

Just in time. The big boulder that stood on top of the cliff was rolling down the cliff face at a terrifying pace. It took a bounce and then hurtled toward us.

"Against the cliff," I shouted. "Flatten yourselves against it."

I hugged the rock face, feeling small rocks bounce off my head and shoulders.

The boulder whooshed past, banged on the rocks below and split into a hundred bits. It was going so fast that most of the pieces buried themselves in the mud; a few rolled so far they reached the water's edge.

"Jeez," I muttered, stepping back on the path to look up. "That was close." I craned my neck; I couldn't see any sign of movement above.

When we reached the top, I was really shaking. I hoped no one would notice.

The Cliff Face

"How'd that rock get from here to there," said Jenny. "It's ten feet from the edge to where it was. You can see the indentation in the ground over there."

The truth was too fantastic to swallow. Someone had deliberately pushed the boulder from its usual place over the edge. There were marks in the ground all the way to the edge.

Sudden chills ran up my spine. I shuddered. It was like someone dropped a piece of ice down my back, and I couldn't shake it free. Someone had tried to kill me! I thought Jenny would be as shaken up as me. When she spoke, I couldn't believe my ears.

"I've got to get back home," said Jenny. "But first I need a shower. Tomorrow we'll try to find out what OLMEC means. We'll start at the library."

"Tomorrow," I shouted. "You are crazy. Someone just tried to kill us. We've got to get the sheriff. And now!"

Jenny looked at me. "You really are a retard. Tell the *sheriff!* You think you'll get that fat old McGlynn down here to look at bits of rock?"

"It was pushed," I protested. "Anyone can see that."

"There isn't even a rock anymore," she said. "You want to make a fuss about a rock falling down a cliff? You think it's big news there's a tunnel that leads to a farmhouse? That's not illegal."

She headed for the shower. "I'll need your bike again to get home. Which towel is mine?"

95

I handed her the red striped one.

"You know cops never listen to kids anyway. So tomorrow we'll start looking for some kind of proof. And listen . . ."

"Yes."

"Oil the bike first, will you, it's kind of hard to pedal."

Girls!

10

Bandit Strikes Out

Jenny was right. I tried to talk to Dad about it next morning, but Rodney had strayed into some poison ivy and had to have medicine and ointment around the clock. Also, the book had reached an important state. Apparently this Emperor Titus, besides all his other tricks, had torn down Solomon's temple in Jerusalem. Boy, he sure was busy making friends. Dad told me all this while rubbing Rodney down with Cortaid.

He dismissed the rock incident as a "freak of nature" —that was what he called it—"a freak of nature." That freak of nature almost squished his son.

"Let me assure you, Jeff Glover," he said, "no one wants to kill you at your age unless it's a seventh-grade teacher." He thought that was hysterical. He turned to Rodney. "Am I right, Rodders?"

"Right, Dad," came the pesky echo.

I didn't tell him about the tunnel because I was afraid he'd ground me.

"Here's five bucks, Jeff," he added. "I'm so far behind now that I can't fix dinner. Get some chicken later from Mrs. Klause at the Chicken Koop for Nguyen and you. I don't think Rodney wants anything much to eat. I'll have a beer."

Jenny arrived at ten. "Bike's better," she said. "Let's try the library first."

I rode her back to Scottsville, arguing all the time. She wouldn't listen. It was another hot summer day. When we leaned the bikes up against the tree she whispered, "But not a word to that nosy Miss Boswell."

We got the usual suspicious looks as we went in. I know I didn't smell because I had put on lots of Dad's cologne. Jenny smelled like a flower store. Her T-shirt had a bunch of women in old-fashioned clothes tied to some railings. It said, "No one's gonna fence us in." Miss Boswell's glasses dropped to the end of their chain when she read it.

However, it was pretty clear that Miss Boswell was a bit leery of Jenny so she didn't hassle us. Being smart has its compensations.

"Olmec" wasn't in any dictionary we could find, and it wasn't in the *Britannica Junior Encyclopaedia* either.

There was an article on olives followed by one on some guy called Jose Joaquim de Olmedo, but nothing in between.

Miss Boswell pushed the cart into the far room. It squeaked, and one of the front wheels flapped from side to side. Jenny followed her.

"May we consult the *Britannica III* please, Miss Boswell?"

"Well, Jennifer, are your hands clean?"

Jenny showed them. I thought Miss Boswell's nose wrinkled a bit; maybe it was my imagination. But she produced the key to the glass bookcase. The *Britannica III* was her pride and joy; so it was kept in the locked display case.

"Remember, Jennifer dear, it cost nine hundred dollars."

"I only want volume seven of the Micropaedia," Jenny said in a phony sweet little girl voice. It worked, and she carried the book to a table. I looked over her shoulder.

"Oklahoma, Old Maid, Omani, oops, too far, Olson, Olmec. Here it is!

"Well what does it say?"

"There's too much to read, but it's a name for pre-Columbian art."

"That's a lot of help. What does Columbus have to do with Loon Lake?"

"Not Columbus, you dope. Way before Columbus.

Olmec art is big sculptures and small stone carvings and pottery. Come on." She closed the book, placed it on the return book shelf and led the way to the door. We sat outside on the porch. Jenny looked at me, then Nguyen. "Don't you get it? Bickerstaffe and those guys are smugglers."

I leaned back against the wall of the library. "That's crazy. There aren't any smugglers now."

"Plenty smugglers in Vietnam," said Nguyen, carefully tying one of his shoelaces. "They bad people."

"This isn't ordinary smugglers," Jenny said. She stopped talking as Mrs. Hill went by. She was the biggest gossip around. We all said, "Hi."

"Why smuggle art," I said. "Why not just buy it?"

"You can't buy it," Jenny replied, getting to her feet. "If you had all the money in the world, you couldn't buy the Mona Lisa, but you could sell it OK."

"But everyone would know it was stolen," I pointed out.

"If you were a collector *and* a crook you wouldn't care. This stuff probably goes to some rich Canadian or is flown out to France."

I stood up and walked over to my bike. "Then why the tunnel?"

Jenny got on the seat of my bike while I steadied it. She held onto my shoulders.

"So it can go from the United States into Canada without customs checks. There's no risk, see? How are you going to explain ten boxes of Olmec art in the trunk of a car? This way is easy. You don't have any risks, and it doesn't have to be carted across the border through the pine forest."

I pushed off; we wobbled, then picked up speed. "So the boxes we saw," I said over my shoulder, "were for the art."

"Smart. You got any money?"

"Five bucks for dinner."

"Head for the ice cream place. You can get a Super Chicken Box for three-fifty later. So that leaves a dollar-fifty, and I've got a dollar seventy-five."

A few minutes later, we entered the ice cream parlor through the screen door. It slammed back with a bang. There were more hanging plants than I remembered from the last visit.

Nguyen felt in his pockets and produced a light green dollar. "Guess Dad threw my shorts and dollar in washer together," he said, grinning.

Jenny ordered a Tin Roof, so Nguyen and I had to settle for cones with single scoops.

"They were pretty lucky with that farmhouse," I said. "I mean it was right above the tunnel."

Jenny slurped ice cream and peanuts from her spoon and looked at me in amazement.

"Boy, it's hard to believe you go to school. It's not a farmhouse," she continued, pouring hot fudge carefully on the top of the vanilla. "It was a dormitory. After the tunnel got five miles long they sank a shaft. That way the workers didn't have to travel five miles to the tunnel entrance and five more to where they were digging." She looked for a napkin. Nguyen pushed one over with a fern printed on it. "See they had to go only a hundred forty feet—straight down."

It all made sense. I licked my cone and thought about it. Bickerstaffe found out about the tunnel when he read Mrs. Mulvenny's book.

"What now?" I said, when she'd finished her Tin Roof. "The sherff?"

"That's a laugh," she said, wiping her mouth. "Do you think Deputy McGlynn could figure it out?"

She got up and headed for the door. "We still don't have any proof."

"What proof do we need?"

"Some art."

She held the screen door open for a lady with a stroller. We didn't know her, but we all said, "Hi." Scottsville is a friendly place. The screen door slammed shut, and the baby in the stroller started to cry. I was about to get my bike when Jenny flung out her arm and jammed me back against the side of the building.

"Jeez," I said, "What's . . ."

"Bickerstaffe," she hissed. "Going into the Abnaki Tavern."

The Abnaki Tavern is the closest thing there is in Scottsville to a "joint." It's open all hours and once a woman was said to have danced there naked. I'd only been in it once when Dad bought beer for his annual fish fry. It was very dark inside, with a bar up at one end and booths at the other. The tavern was a very narrow building, and in that light I don't suppose anyone saw much of the woman who danced.

"Let's find out what he's up to," Jenny said. "Is there a back entrance?"

"You can't go in there," I hissed; "it's men only and no kids."

Jenny wasn't listening. Behind the tavern was a fenced yard full of junk. She was already slipping through the fence while Nguyen and I leaned our bikes against it.

"Stay here, Nguyen," I told him. "I'll try to get her to see sense."

Nguyen nodded. He never argued, and that sure helped in a situation like this.

The back door to the tavern was open and the screen door was unlocked. Right then we almost ran into Bickerstaffe. He was just sitting down in the next to the last booth. Fortunately he was facing the other way. The back of the booth was pretty high. I could make out the top of a man's head facing him. It was too dark to see much more. Bickerstaffe's derby was hanging from a hook beside the booth.

"I can't hear a thing," whispered Jenny.

"I'm not surprised," I said. The juke box was blaring country music away down by the bar. Finally it stopped.

I hate those records where everyone is on the verge of tears.

"I'm going in," she said.

"You can't do that," I said. "You'll get arrested."

"If we can get in the booth behind them we might hear what they're saying. Come on."

She pulled me by the arm so there was nothing for it but to go. We slid into the last booth.

It wasn't easy to tune out all the other noises. The juke box stayed off, which helped. There was occasional loud laughter from the bar, and there was a lot of smoke from cigarettes, which made my eyes sting.

Luckily for us, the two men had to talk pretty loudly to make themselves heard.

Bickerstaffe was complaining; that didn't surprise me. "I let you into the business of the tunnel," he was saying. "Before that you always had the problem of getting the stuff across. Three years of trouble-free business for you, peanuts for me. I made more when I was in the carpentry trade."

"You'll do all right," the other man said, in a familiar tone. "Especially for an ex-jail bird. They'd deport you if they knew. Some of the smaller pieces are worth a hundred grand apiece. You get ten percent."

I heard a match strike in a sudden silence; then the voice continued. "You've put away quite a bit for that vine-covered cottage in Devon, haven't you?"

"It's Surrey, not Devon."

"Whatever."

"And I've got to put up with that old bat, Mrs. M. Do you know what that's like?"

"Drink your beer."

"I don't like Yank beer. It's no taste to it. She spends all her time playing that organ and working on her income taxes. You can't claim anything on taxes after seven years anyhow. She's only reached 1939. Why don't this place serve Guinness?"

There was silence. Then the second man spoke. "Try a Bud Lite instead."

Bickerstaffe snorted. "Flat cider! What about those kids, Deitz? They're on to us I tell you. They're always poking around."

"I'll handle them," replied Deitz in a cold voice. "Mr. Vadillo gave me new orders." Jenny nudged me in the ribs. "I've tried to warn them off. I might be forced to a more permanent solution."

Bickerstaffe sounded agitated. "I don't want no trouble. I won't stand for any messy stuff."

"Relax, Isaac," Deitz said. "You concentrate on the job in hand. Now I've got to go. Just be ready to go tomorrow night. Here's the list. Eight items."

That was enough for us. We shot out of the back door like snakes near a mongoose. Nguyen was holding the bikes and looking a bit anxious.

"Now we've got the proof for Deputy McGlynn," I said. "We can tell him . . ." My voice trailed away.

"That we were in a tavern spying on people. Oh sure," said Jenny.

She was right of course. And somewhere deep down I knew what was coming next. It did! "We've got to be there tomorrow night," she added. "To get proof. Something that will get McGlynn away from food for a while."

"Food," I said, remembering. "We've got to go to the Chicken Koop."

"See you tomorrow night then. I'll borrow your bike?"

Nguyen rode me around to the Chicken Koop which wasn't easy on a Huffy dirt bike. Deputy McGlynn was just coming out with a Party Barrel under one arm. That was enough for eight people. He had the usual cigar butt between yellow teeth and just nodded as we went in.

We hadn't quite got enough for the Super Box. However, Mrs. Klause let us have it anyway, and she gave us rolls in place of slaw, which I hate. We left the chicken in the back cabin and went for a swim.

Dad was sitting in front of his word processor when we got back. Rodney was watching a ball game. Every so often, without taking his eyes off his screen, Dad would squirt Rodney with his medication.

Nguyen and I said "Good night," and went up to the back cabin. Then I remembered the rowboat, so we had to go down the narrow path and get out of the canoe and paddle across Loon Lake and put both boats in our dock for the night.

"I ready for chicken now," said Nguyen, as we finally entered the back cabin. "Could eat a horse . . . Oh boy!" He pulled up short.

"What is it?" I said, moving past him.

"We had visitors."

The living room was a shambles. Bits of chicken and rolls were scattered from one end of the room to the other.

"One visitor," I said. "One raccoon, name of Bandit."

"Bandit steal his last food," said Nguyen, from beside the sofa.

"That's right," I said. "Tomorrow we find his secret entrance and seal it up."

"Not necessary," said Nguyen, pointing behind the sofa.

There was Bandit, fat and fast asleep.

"Don't touch him," I said, "or you'll scare him. He might bite.

"Think not," said Nguyen.

I needn't have worried. Nothing would ever spook Bandit again. When I knelt down to examine him, I saw that his mouth was wide open and his eyes frozen. And you didn't have to be a vet to know he hadn't choked on a chicken bone.

11

The Rats

We stared at Bandit, fascinated. His lips were pulled way back so we could see all his teeth; they were white and sharp, especially the fangs.

"What happened?" said Nguyen.

"It's pretty obvious," I replied. "While we were down at the lake someone poisoned the chicken. Bandit sneaked in and ate the lot, scattering the chicken and the box all over the floor."

"He a pretty messy eater."

"Not anymore," I said, looking at Bandit's body. I was really scared now. First the rock on the cliff, now the chicken. Deitz hadn't wasted much time.

"Come on," I said, "Let's clean up the mess.

It took a while. First we buried Bandit at the edge of the clearing.

"Major Nelson be happy about this," said Nguyen glumly, as we scattered pine leaves and cones over the grave.

"He sure would be, but I wouldn't give him the satisfaction of knowing," I answered, placing a rock on the grave as a headstone. "This time I am going to the sheriff."

"He say chicken bone kill Bandit."

"Not if they analyze the chicken. They'll find the poison."

"Take a long time. Will have to be sent to Manchester. Also will tell smugglers what's happening."

"You're right," I admitted, leading the way back to the cabin. "If we spook them, they'll simply quit."

The next day dragged by. We swam in Loon Lake, paddled the canoe to the boathouse and fished off the dock. In the afternoon Nguyen pulled out his Mah Jongg set. By dinnertime, he had over a hundred thousand points; I had sixty.

We ate with Dad in the main cabin. It was soup. I had Cheddar cheese and Nguyen clam chowder. Dad was surprised we stayed around until ten o'clock. Neither Nguyen or I liked being in the back cabin any longer than necessary.

We'd locked the back cabin up securely, but it was a relief to hear the sound of my bike pulling up outside.

Jenny was shaken up when she heard about Bandit. "They play rough. Why didn't you keep the body. Dr. Karr could have done a postmortem on it."

"We buried him," I said shortly.

She nodded. "OK. Keep your fur on."

For once she didn't have a T-shirt with a message on it. She had a dark blue ski cap on and a black sweater and dark jeans. "Camouflage," she said seeing me eyeing her. "Get your darkest clothes on."

From her backpack, Jenny pulled out a can of Off.

"Spray this on yourselves," she ordered. "It's going to be rough waiting around in the Swamp."

It sure was. If we hadn't known Bickerstaffe was coming, we would have been long gone. It was pretty dark too. There were black clouds that kept rushing across in front of the moon. Tomorrow we'd have a thunderstorm for sure.

Mosquitoes like damp places and people sitting in canoes. Tonight they had both. We were sitting targets in the boat. Every so often, you get a skeeter that loves Off, and once I smacked one so hard the canoe rocked.

"Got him," I whispered.

"It's a she," Jenny muttered. "Males don't bite. And don't make such a racket."

That was just like Jenny Weber. Orders and lectures, orders and lectures. Nguyen was probably laughing to himself; he seemed to be immune to skeeters.

There were the usual scares. Once a water snake

slithered off an island and up my paddle into the boat. He, or she, was more scared than we were, but I discovered Jenny was no friend of snakes.

"What time is it?" asked Jenny, to cover the embarrassment.

I reached for the flashlight. Over the end was a piece of cloth so the beam would be diffused. Shining it on my watch, I saw it was almost midnight. "Almost twelve."

She sniffed. "That Bickerstaffe sure is corny doing things at midnight. He sees too many—"

"Wait!" I interrupted, "listen!"

In the distance was the unmistakable sound of the small trolling engine.

"Someone's coming all right," she agreed. "Heading toward us."

The engine grew louder and closer. We froze listening. Then the noise veered off, then sounded much nearer.

"Going to the tunnel," I whispered. "Let's go."

"All we want," said Jenny, "is one piece of art or whatever it is. That's all the proof we need."

The boat ahead was weaving its way around the grassy islands. Since we knew its destination we were in a good spot—well concealed, but near enough to the entrance.

The water fell from our paddles. An owl hooted nearby; then something flew past my face, leathery wings flapping. I ducked instinctively, hearing a small squeaking noise. A bat! I hate them. One time, Rodney was almost bitten by one until Mom flattened it with a towel. Dad had to kill it. It still made me shudder to think of, he drowned it in a garbage bag full of water.

Crouching lower in the canoe, I wiped my hands on my jeans. A breeze sprang up and thousands of reeds whispered and bowed around us. The canoe edged its way smoothly across a narrow channel, cut through a stand of rushes, and there in front of us were the ferns concealing the entrance to the tunnel.

There was no sign of the boat. "Must be well inside now," said Jenny. "Let's go."

We paddled slowly, not daring to shine the flashlight. With our paddles we could feel the sides, so it wasn't too bad. We couldn't even see the water, but every so often there was the slap of water against the canoe or the walls. Once something fell or jumped into the water with a splash.

"Rats," whispered Jenny, "and we were swimming in it."

"Why can't we hear the engine?" I murmured. "Let's stop and listen."

Then we did hear the engine. It was distant but seemed to be getting louder. The next thing I realized was that the boat wasn't ahead of us.

"They've outsmarted us," I said, my voice echoing around us. "They're behind us."

Bickerstaffe and Deitz had waited until we'd entered the tunnel and then followed us in.

"Paddle," I said, "paddle."

The noise of the engine was deafening now, banging around the tunnel.

Nguyen and I were really paddling, but the power-boat was gaining fast, then abruptly, the canoe smacked up against something; pitching me out, and throwing Jenny and Nguyen to the bottom of the canoe.

"The gate," I gasped coming up for air and spitting out vile tasting water, "it's closed."

A light filled the tunnel. Bickerstaffe, without his derby hat, was aiming a spotlight at us. There were two other men in the boat, but I couldn't make out anything more as I clambered back into the canoe. The engine was turned off.

"Well, look what we've caught," said Bickerstaffe. "Should look where you're going. Open the grille, Maddox."

The second man was younger, with red hair and a sandy moustache. He waded past us, and felt for the bolt. The grille opened.

"Tie them to it," said the third man. I could tell from the voice it was Deitz. "And make them secure."

Maddox took a rope and threaded it through the grille. It wasn't that tight.

"You're too soft," said Deitz, wading over. He tugged

on the ropes, and I felt them cutting into my arms. "Like that."

He looked at us. "The ropes are wet now. When they dry, they'll pull tighter."

He waded back into his boat. "The more you struggle now, the worse it'll be for you when they do."

The three men were back in the boat, and the engine puttered into life.

As Deitz passed us, he said, "We'll be back in a couple of hours. Don't leave without us." He gave a laugh. "By then I'll have thought up some accident for you."

The boat moved away up the tunnel, the light bobbing along the walls. For a long time, we heard the engine throbbing into the distance, its echoes reverberating off the walls.

I tugged the rope around my wrists. There wasn't the slightest give. A strangled sound came from Jenny.

"What is it?"

"The rope's around my throat. If you pull it, I can't breathe."

I froze. "No one move," I said. "We're trapped but good."

"What they do with us?" asked Nguyen.

"Guess," I replied. "You heard Deitz. We've seen all their faces. They know we can recognize them. What would you do?"

"They won't kill us, will they?" asked Jenny. "I mean they'll hang them for that. They'd be crazy to do it."

"They don't have to kill us," I pointed out. "All they have to do is leave us here. An accident. We'd die anyway. First starvation, then . . . then . . ."

There was a sudden splash nearby as something swam in the black tunnel water.

"Then the rats," said Jenny, in a whisper. "Then the rats."

12

Hunted

It was a long time before we saw the light or heard the engine of the smugglers' boat coming back toward us. I was numb from the waist down. My hands were clenched around an iron bar supporting my weight because every move I made caused the rope to bite into Jenny's throat. When I tried to flex any muscles, they hurt.

The spotlight was focused directly in my eyes so I couldn't see anything.

"Well," said Bickerstaffe, "now what?"

"Leave them," said Deitz.

"We can't do that," protested Bickerstaffe. "That would be murder."

"That's right," said the other man. "We don't want any part of it."

There was a harsh laugh. "Not scared of a few kids are you?"

'No killing," shouted Bickerstaffe. "I won't 'ave it. Smuggling's one thing, murder's another."

"Then why did you poison our chicken?" I demanded.

The light went out. "What chickens is he talking about?" demanded Bickerstaffe.

A match flared; Deitz was lighting his pipe. The match cast shadows up his face. "Not chickens, Isaac, chicken. Last night I flavored their dinners. Not enough to kill them. Enough to keep them out of the way." He pulled on his pipe, the tobacco glowed red in the bowl. "I must say I was surprised to see them."

There was a long silence. Finally Deitz spoke. "Well, I'm waiting."

"I'm thinking."

"A new experience for you, Isaac."

Bickerstaffe switched on the light, aiming it away from us at the wall of the tunnel. "I've got a friend to 'elp me, don't forget that." Everybody could see clearly now. The butler had a revolver in one hand. "First we gets out of here. Then we take them up north. Up to Quebec. They could wander for weeks around Lake St. Francis."

There was a laugh from Deitz. "And they die of exposure there instead of here."

"Untie them," ordered Bickerstaffe. "I've got the gun. I'll decide what we do. I don't want no killing."

117

"You're the boss, Isaac," said Deitz. "But I don't think the Consortium is going to like it."

Maddox was already in the water untying us. Jenny fell into the water, and he had to help her up. She was coughing and holding her neck.

"Do what he says," Maddox said to us in a low voice.

"In the boat and look sharp about it," Bickerstaffe said. "Maddox, tie their hands behind them. And fasten a loop over their ankles. We don't want no heroics."

There was plenty of room in the well of the boat where the packing cases had been stored. We sat there, arms, and legs tied. Maddox seemed OK; he didn't pull them tight. Deitz started the trolling motor, and slowly we edged along the tunnel. The light was pointing behind and up so we could see everything. The walls were much closer than they had been in the canoe and once or twice we seemed to scrape bottom. Deitz controlled the motor and steered.

Since the light shone behind us, there was no need to turn it off until the end of the tunnel was a few feet ahead. When Deitz put out the light and emptied his pipe, the boat was already sliding between the ferns into the Swamp.

The moon was hidden by clouds for a few seconds so it was pitch dark for an instant. There was a loud splash and the boat rocked from side to side and drifted. The engine was silent.

When the clouds passed, Deitz was gone.

" 'Ere," exclaimed Bickerstaffe in alarm. "Where's he gone?"

He found out immediately. Deitz came up out of the water on the far side of the boat, grabbing Bickerstaffe by the leg, toppling him backwards into the Swamp.

Maddox tried to get Bickerstaffe's revolver as he fell, but it dropped into the water with a plop. Then Maddox lost his footing, the boat tipped, rocked back, and began taking on water. As Maddox went overboard, the shifting weight flipped the boat over and flung Nguyen, Jenny and me over the side.

The next thing I saw was Deitz holding Bickerstaffe's face under the water. My head bobbed up; the water was less than three feet deep. Despite being tied hand and foot, I found my footing and stood up. Nguyen and Jenny were stuck in a bed of reeds, but their heads were above water.

Maddox hadn't done a good job of tying me up. The rope around my wrists was so loose, it almost slid off when I wrestled with it. The ankles were more trouble, but once my hands were loose, it wasn't much trouble to untie them.

Deitz was still holding Bickerstaffe's face under water. The butler was still struggling but less violently. In seconds he would be dead.

My hand brushed against something solid. It was a paddle from the boat. I seized it and waded a few steps until I was behind Deitz.

I brought the paddle down on his head with all my strength. It gave a loud crack and split across the handle.

Deitz gave a bellow of rage but let go of Bicker-staffe. The butler slid under the water. Deitz now charged after me.

The water made running next to impossible, but Deitz had more trouble than I did. Ahead of me was an island, a long sandy spit with spiky grass. I scrambled onto it and ran headlong. Just behind me came Deitz. The spit was less than twenty yards long. I dashed the whole length and flung myself as far out into the channel beyond it as I could. Then I waded ashore on another island and broke through the reeds at the far end.

Deitz was gaining fast; I could hear the breath being forced from his mouth.

A root caught my foot and slammed me to the ground. My face was buried in sand and tiny shell fragments.

"Get up, get up," a voice deep inside me said. "Run, run!"

Deitz was less than ten feet behind me. "Don't look back," the voice said. "Get into the water."

I zigzagged and crashed through the reeds into the water. Deitz plunged in after me.

In the distance, I heard the sound of an engine. At first it was no louder than the trolling motor, but it was rapidly became louder. Ahead was a bright core of light.

Hunted

The next island was longer and wider than most. I crawled out of the water, staggered to my feet and ran.

The engine roar was much nearer, and it was far too loud for a powerboat. I looked up. Flying in from the east was a helicopter, a bright spotlight shining down into the Swamp.

At that moment Deitz flung himself full-length and tripped me. I fell with him on top of me; we rolled over and over and slid back into the water.

Deitz lost his grip. The water was no longer clear; mud and broken reeds made it impossible to see. I clung to the roots of a huge mass of rushes until I thought my lungs would burst. When I came to the surface, sputtering and coughing, there was no sign of Deitz. A helicopter was hovering above, a searchlight aimed directly at me. A second helicopter had landed on an island a hundred yards away. Men with rifles were leaping from it.

Then my legs gave way; down I went, the water closed above me again.

When I floated back to consciousness, my body was one solid ache. A man in aviator glasses was stuffing his flying jacket under my head.

"Drink this," he said, lifting me up and putting a small metal flask to my lips. A hot liquid poured down my throat. I coughed several times.

"OK. Now lie still."

The helicopter had landed on the island; he walked to it and shouted something to the pilot. The rotors began to turn. He waved it away and came back to me. There was a loud crack and the rotor blades whirled around flattening the grass and reeds. Flocks of small birds rose into the air, startled by the sound. The water was covered with tiny waves.

When it was gone, the man spoke to me again.

"You must have swallowed half the Swamp. Still you gave most of it back. There'll be a couple of powerboats here soon. You want another drink?"

"No, thanks," I said trying to sit up.

He helped me. "My name's Al by the way."

"Jeff," I said.

"I know."

"What about Nguyen and Jenny?"

"They're fine. We're keeping them safe while we round up your friends."

Two men waded across the channel; one was Maddox.

"You got Maddox then?"

"I wouldn't quite put it that way." He grinned. "Joe's been on this case for two years. He's with the FBI. He followed you on your little trip to Canada the other day. This is really his show."

Maddox squatted beside me. "Sorry I couldn't give you much help in the tunnel. We had to get the smugglers on the Canadian end first.

"I'm the guy who left the note at the house," he added. "I suppose you saw it and figured it out."

"Olmec, seventeen July," I said.

"Right. Come on, here's your transport out of here."

A motorboat was edging into the channel near us. Nguyen and Jenny were sitting in the stern covered in blankets. Al helped me to my feet; I was unsteady, and Maddox gave me his arm.

"I thought you were one of the gang," I told him. "Sorry."

He grinned. "So did they, Jeff, or I'd be floating face down in the tunnel. Simon Deitz is a dangerous man. A real ugly customer."

I sat in the bow of the boat with Al. "We'll take you and your brother home first. Then Jenny. She's really going to get it when she gets home."

"She's awful quiet," I said. "Do her parents have to know?"

"Oh, yes," Al replied. "There's no way around that. You see, Jeff, my full name is Al Weber."

I looked at his face, then turned to look at Jenny. She managed a weak smile.

"You're Jenny's dad? Boy, that's something."

"We're going to have a long heart to heart when we get home that young lady and I."

The boat eased out of the channel and picked up speed through the neck into Loon's Lake. I glanced at Mr. Weber's face in the moonlight. You know, he didn't look that mad. I'd say he looked kind of proud.

13

New Lamps for Old

For the next three days we were heroes. Customs' officers interviewed us, lawyers took statements and depositions, and Major Nelson congratulated us and showed us some slides he'd taken during the Korean War.

Dad wasn't quite so pleased. Nguyen and I were grounded and confined to the back cottage for two weeks. No exceptions. Most of the time we played Mah Jongg and watched Channel Three on TV.

Rodney cashed in on our fame. He got to ride across the lake in a helicopter with Dad. He brought our meals up from the main cottage and never stopped talking about how high the 'coptor went and how small everything looked from up there. His poison ivy had cleared up, and he was back using words like "sweet" and calling everyone he didn't like a "dip."

Rodney was our source of local news. Dad's book was just about done. There were seven hundred pages on a guy who'd been emperor for two years. That was almost a page a day! What if the guy had ruled as long as Queen Victoria?

As for Bickerstaffe, he was gone. Vanished. But Deitz was in jail and Mr. Vadillo. There were others too we'd never met. Mr. Weber told Rodney that the Mexican Government wanted Deitz when we'd finished with him. He figured there wouldn't be time for Deitz to serve both sentences.

Jenny was grounded for a whole month and was allowed one five-minute call a day to us. She was going to get a ten-speed bike though, because Mr. Weber figured it would keep her out of trouble.

About a week after all the excitement had died down. Dad came up to the back cabin. He walked around as if he was nervous. He cleared his throat a couple of times, the way he does when he has a Big Announcement.

"It's pretty clear that I'm partly to blame for what happened," he said. "Lack of supervision. That's obvious." He sat on the sofa, banged a cushion a couple of times, then got up. "So I'm only going to work on the book in the mornings. In the afternoons, I shall be free." He fumbled in his pockets, pulled out his pipe and began stuffing tobacco in the bowl.

"That's great, Dad," I said, "we can go fishing today. It's almost time for your annual fish fry."

"Well, not today, Jeff," he said quickly. "There's someone from Yale University Press coming to talk about a book on Pizarro and the Incas."

A jet of flame shot out of his butane lighter the way it always did; he quickly adjusted it and lit his pipe.

"Of course, I'm not going to do it. It's only talk."

"He come a long way just to talk," Nguyen pointed out.

"Ah, well, publishers spend lots of money traveling and entertaining," Dad said. "That's why writers don't make much."

He moved across to the door. "Even if I did do it," he added, "I would only work on it in the mornings. Absolutely."

After he had gone, I looked at Nguyen. "I thought Titus was enough, now it's Pizarro."

Together we walked down to Loon Lake just in time to see Rodney and his equally pesty friend Adrian getting into the rowboat. Rodney had a new fishing rod with a fancy reel on it.

"Where'd you get the reel?" I asked him.

"Bought it," he said, looking very pleased with himself. "It's a Daiawa 7000C. Got a skirted spool spinning reel. Cost sixty bucks."

"You don't have sixty cents," I said. "So where'd you get it from?"

Rodney practiced a cast from the shore; the hook got caught in his hair.

"Do so," he muttered. "I sold that old rock Nguyen found in the lake."

Nguyen had to help him get the hook out of his hair. "Who bought it?"

"Some guy," said Rodney, rewinding his line. "Some guy who collects carved bits of granite. I didn't even know it was granite."

I asked the question even though I knew the answer.

"Was he a short, fat man with an English accent? I mean did he talk like Mr. French in *Family Affair*?"

"I dunno. Never saw it."

And with that he climbed into the boat and shoved off.

I turned to Nguyen. "Rodney gave Bickerstaffe a piece of Olmec art probably worth about fifty thousands bucks for a fishing rod. Jeez!"

I looked at Rodney struggling with his oar. "I just know I was never seven years old," I said. "I couldn't have been. No way!"

Nguyen just grinned at me. "Bickerstaffe got all the Guinness he want now, that's for sure."

In the distance, I heard the piercing cry of a loon.